DOCTOR WHO –
THE CAVES OF ANDROZANI

DOCTOR WHO
THE CAVES OF ANDROZANI

Based on the BBC television serial by Robert Holmes by
arrangement with the British Broadcasting Corporation

ROBERT HOLMES

Number 92
in the
Doctor Who Library

A TARGET BOOK

published by
the Paperback Division of
W. H. ALLEN & Co. PLC

A Target Book
Published in 1985
By the Paperback Division of
W. H. Allen & Co. PLC
44 Hill Street, London W1X 8LB

First published in Great Britain by
W. H. Allen & Co. Ltd 1984

The BBC producer of *The Caves of Androzani* was John Nathan-Turner, the
director was Graeme Harper.

Printed and bound in Great Britain by
Anchor Brendon Ltd. Tiptree, Essex.

ISBN 0 426 19959 6

CONTENTS

1

Androzani Minor Revisited

Twin planets orbiting each other in space – one large, one relatively small – Androzani Major and Androzani Minor were two of the five planets that made up the Sirius system. Androzani Major was civilised, even industrialised, the home of an industrial conglomerate powerful enough to influence government – a complete contrast to Androzani Minor, which was uncolonised and very largely uninhabited, an unattractive planet of desert rocky plains and seething mud volcanoes.

Yet this barren little planet held the key to a power and prosperity far greater than that of its richer twin. Androzani Minor was the source – the only source – of spectrox, the most valuable drug in the universe. Spectrox was the reason for the savage guerrilla war being waged in the cave system beneath the surface of Androzani Minor. And this spectrox was soon to have a devastating effect on that mysterious traveller in space and time known as the Doctor, and his current companion, a girl called Perpugilliam Brown – Peri for short.

A wheezing groaning sound shattered the silence of the rocky desert of Androzani Minor and an incongruous square blue-shape appeared.

Two figures emerged into the glare and heat of the sun. The Doctor, now in his fifth incarnation, was a slight, fair-haired figure with a pleasant open face, and an air of mildly-bemused curiosity. He wore the garb of an Edwardian cricketer: striped trousers, fawn blazer with red piping, a cricket sweater bordered in red and white, and an open-necked shirt. There was a sprig of celery in his lapel.

His companion, Peri, was an attractive American girl, her piquant features framed in short dark hair. She wore pink shorts and open-necked pink shirt.

The Doctor and Peri stood by the TARDIS for a moment, looking around them. They were on a bare rocky plain, ringed by distant mountains. Scattered about the plain were great twisted monoliths, pillars of rock carved into weird shapes by the scouring of the desert winds.

Peri surveyed the barren prospect. 'The tide's out!'

The Doctor seemed lost in thought. 'Mmm?'

'When you said sand, I thought maybe I could take a dip.'

'You're a little late, Peri. It's about a billion years since there's been any sea on Androzani Minor.'

'You're such a pain, Doctor!'

The Doctor nodded absent-mindedly. 'Come on!'

'Come on where?' thought Peri. She followed him across the desert.

The Doctor strode happily onwards, glancing keenly about him, as alert and interested as if they'd been visiting one of the great beauty spots of the universe. That was one of the Doctor's most endearing and aggravating characteristics, thought Peri. He was interested in everything.

'Doctor, this place is just unbelievable!'

The remark hadn't been intended as praise, but the Doctor took it as such, smiling at her appreciation.

'The old place hasn't changed at all. Still nothing but sand!'

Peri spotted something gleaming at her feet. She stopped and picked up a handful of greenish globules. 'Doctor, look!'

'What?'

'Glass!'

The Doctor took the globules from her and peered at them. 'Almost, anyway. It's fused silica.' Peri's earlier remark made its way through into his consciousness and he added indignantly, 'I'm not a pain!' He began searching the area around them. 'Here's some more of the stuff. Now, why would anyone want to come to a place like this?'

'Why indeed?' thought Peri. 'Who says anyone has, apart from us?'

'These patches of silica were fused by the rocket pods of some kind of spacecraft.' He studied the globules more closely. 'Too small for interstellar travel, I think, so it obviously came from the twin planet, Androzani Major. The interesting question is – why?'

'Maybe someone wanted some sand to make some glass so they could blow a new vacuum tube for their reticular vector gauge?' Peri suggested helpfully.

'Sarcasm is not your strong point, Peri. If I were you I'd stick to – aha! What have we here?'

The Doctor rushed off to study two tracks stretching away into the distance like wobbling train-lines.

'Aha!' mimicked Peri. She followed him. 'All right, Doctor, I'm looking. *Why* am I looking?'

'These tracks were left by a monoskid. You can see the deep furrow where it left the ship and the shallow one where it returned.'

'Or vice versa?'

The Doctor shook his head with irritating certainty. 'No, no, no. You can see where the light track sometimes crosses the heavy one. So, someone came here with a heavily laden monoskid, unloaded it somewhere, and then returned to the ship.'

'So, you got a merit badge in tracking when you were a boy scout. I'm suitably impressed, Doctor. Can we go now?'

'One moment,' said the Doctor absently. 'Yes, it looks as if the tracks lead to those caves over there.'

Peri followed the direction of his gaze. They were standing in a sort of shallow basin, its walls formed from eroded rock. On the far side of the basin, the

4

low walls were pierced by a number of openings – presumably the caves to which the Doctor had referred.

The Doctor began heading determinedly towards them.

Peri hurried after him. 'Is this wise, I ask myself?' she muttered. 'Oh well!'

As they approached the caves the Doctor said suddenly, 'Blow-holes!'

'What?'

'Now we're nearer, you can see. They're not caves, they're blow-holes!'

'Same difference, surely?'

'Not to a speleogist,' said the Doctor reprovingly. 'And not if you get stuck in one of those things at high tide.'

'High tide? I thought you said . . .'

'A figure of speech.' Always eager to impart knowledge, the Doctor explained. 'The core of this planet is superheated primeval mud. When its orbit takes it close to Androzani Major, there's a sort of tidal effect . . .'

Peri shuddered. 'I get the picture. Mud baths for everyone! Well, it makes a change from lava, I suppose.'

The Doctor frowned, reproving her frivolity. 'Presumably that's why this planet has never been properly colonised. Androzani Major on the other hand is getting quite developed – at least, it was the last time I passed this way.'

'When was that?'

'I don't remember, but I'm pretty sure it wasn't in the future.'

'You're a very confusing person to be with, Doctor, you know that?'

The Doctor looked a little crestfallen. 'I tried keeping a diary once – not chronologically of course. But the trouble with time travel is, one never seems to find the time!'

They had reached the nearest of the cave mouths by now, and with this, the Doctor popped inside.

Helplessly, Peri followed him.

Although the Doctor and Peri didn't realise it, they were not alone in the cave system. Not far away, a squad of soldiers was hard at work.

They wore silver-grey uniforms with protective helmets, and carried machine-pistols. Their bodies were slung with cross-belts holding cartridges and grenades. Two of them were using instruments to measure distances travelled and the depth of the caves.

The survey of this particular section was virtually finished, and the senior soldier, Trooper Boze, gathered up his gear and moved on ahead to the next position.

By the time he had reached a place he considered satisfactory, the rest of his party were a considerable way behind him, out of sight.

Boze set up his instruments in the new cave and began taking preliminary readings. Absorbed in the familiar routine, he failed to notice the massive shape that stirred in the shadows of the cave. Rearing up, it moved stealthily towards him.

It was quite close by the time Boze heard the grating of its claws on the rock and swung around. He saw red eyes, slavering fangs, great savage claws reaching out for him.

Boze screamed – and the creature lunged forward, smashing him to the ground.

The rest of the survey-party heard Boze's screams, unslung their weapons and hurried to the rescue, guns blazing. But it was too late. By the time they arrived, Boze was not only dead but half-eaten, and the cave creature had disappeared . . .

The caves of Androzani were truly an astonishing sight, thought Peri. No mere holes in the ground, they consisted of a series of interlinked caves and galleries, large and small, leading ever deeper into the depths of the planet.

The cave through which they were walking now was immense, like a great cathedral. They moved between pillars of twisted rock resembling strange alien sculpture. The whole place was lit with an eerie greenish light.

Peri looked around her in wonder. 'Quite a place, Doctor. Where's the light coming from?'

The Doctor waved towards the walls. 'Natural phosphorescence. There's a luminous crystalline material in these walls.' He ran his fingers along the surface. 'It's polished, smooth as glass.'

Peri wandered to the other side of the cave,

feeling the walls. 'Which reminds me why we came here, Doctor. And it wasn't to go miles and miles into – ' She screamed as her feet slid from under her and she toppled sideways into darkness.

'Be careful not to slip,' called the Doctor rather belatedly. He hurried over to her.

In fact, Peri hadn't fallen very far. She was lodged in a deep crevice in the rocks – a crevice that seemed to be filled with a sort of giant puff-ball. She thrashed about trying to free herself from the sticky white filaments and only succeeded in getting ever more entangled.

The Doctor peered down into the crevice. 'Keep still, Peri!' He studied her situation for a moment. 'All right, now try to straighten up. That's it, reach out and give me your hand.'

Disentangling herself, Peri staggered to her feet and reached for the Doctor's outstretched hand.

'That's it,' he said encouragingly. 'Now then, up you come.' The Doctor could exert astonishing strength when he chose, and Peri found herself heaved bodily out of the crevice.

Her bare legs were covered with sticky white filaments. Frantically she brushed them away. 'Ugh, it's horrid! What is it?'

The Doctor brushed some of the filaments from her shoulders. 'I'm not sure.' He sniffed at a fragment of the stuff between his fingers. 'It's not edible by the smell of it.' He wiped his hands on his coat. 'Probably quite harmless.'

Peri winced as she rubbed the remainder of the stuff from her legs. 'It's stinging!'

'Yes,' said the Doctor thoughtfully. 'Well, whatever it is, don't fall into any more of it!'

He moved on. Peri made a face at his retreating back and followed.

Soon they emerged from the caves and into a rift in the planetary surface, a canyon so deep and so narrow that there was very little sense of being outdoors again, though the occasional shaft of sunlight pierced down through the misty gloom. The floor was lined with oddly-shaped monoliths. It was, thought Peri, rather like walking through some strange gallery of alien sculptures.

She glanced at the Doctor. 'Why do you wear a stick of celery in your lapel?'

'Why? Does it offend you?'

'No, just curious.'

'I'm allergic to certain gases in the Praxsis range of the spectrum.'

'How does the celery help?'

'If the gas is present, the celery turns purple.'

'Then what do you do?'

'I eat the celery,' said the Doctor simply. 'If nothing else, I'm sure it's good for my teeth.'

The cleft ended in another cave-entrance, and soon they were moving through the darkness lit only by the greenish glow from the walls.

In a cave not far away, a small group of tough-looking characters was waiting amidst a pile of crates.

One was dozing, his head nodding on his chest. A couple of others were playing dice. Two others were wrangling half-heartedly, more to pass the time than anything else.

They were tough-looking, hard-bitten characters, naturally enough, since they were gun-runners. They wore black berets and grimy coveralls, decorated with a variety of military accessories. All five were armed to the teeth, their bodies slung about with machine-pistols, cartridges and gas grenades.

The larger of the two wrangling men was Stotz, the leader of the party, good-looking in a villainous kind of way. His longish hair was held back with a black headband and he sported a short ragged beard.

Krelper, his number two, was a seedy depressed-looking character with a scrabby moustache. As usual, Krelper was whining. 'Where are the droids then? Those dummies should have been here yesterday.'

Stotz yawned. 'The last time we made a drop we had to wait three days. So what? Relax and enjoy it. It beats picking chacaws.'

Chacaws were a fiercely-spiked fruit grown on the penal plantations of Androzani Major. The bodies of chacaw pickers were very soon a mass of scar tissue.

'Chacaws?' sneered Krelper. 'I don't pick chacaws, Stotz. I've never been confined. You know why? Because I'm smart!'

Stotz grinned evilly. 'You smart? Krelper, the wind whistles through your ears!'

'Yeah?' said Krelper truculently. 'Well, listen – '

Stotz held up his hand, interrupting him. 'Look! Someone's coming!' He pointed to the autogard, a revolving scanner-globe mounted on a small base. The globe was glowing brightly, signalling movement close by.

'Should be the 'droids,' said Krelper happily. 'Come on everyone, belt-plates.'

The gun-runners began clapping round magnetic plates to the buckles of their belts.

Stotz grabbed the autogard, collapsing it. 'It could also be the Army. Let's get out of sight until we're sure.'

Snatching up weapons and equipment, the gun-runners moved to the end of the gallery, taking cover behind scattered rocks.

Minutes later, the Doctor and Peri came into the gallery.

Peri looked at the pile of crates. 'Well, well, well! End of trail.'

The Doctor went over to the nearest crate, unclipped the fastenings and lifted the lid. He saw a row of stubby weapons, still covered in thick packing-grease. 'Gas carbines.'

Peri opened another crate. It was filled with shiny red plastic cylinders. 'Bombs?'

The Doctor came over and took one out, tossing it in his hand like the cricket ball it resembled. 'Grenades – poison volatisers.'

11

To Peri's relief, the Doctor replaced the grenade. 'Nasty little objects, aren't they?' He studied the crates. 'There must be enough weapons here to equip a small army.'

The Doctor saw a pair of black and yellow dice on the ground and picked them up.

Peri looked around the cave. 'What do you make of it, Doctor? You said nobody lives here.'

The Doctor studied the dice in the palm of his hand. 'I was wrong, then. These dice are still warm.'

'Listen!' said Peri suddenly.

They heard booted feet clattering rapidly towards them.

'Quickly, over here,' said the Doctor.

But he was too late.

Suddenly the gallery was filling up with silver-uniformed soldiers. The soldiers ran towards them, weapons in their hands.

Peri looked at the Doctor. 'Now what do we do?'

The Doctor sighed. 'Surrender,' he said wearily and raised his hands.

2

Spectrox War

General Chellak sat at his desk in the Androzani Minor Army Base HQ, grappling with the endless paperwork that always comes with high command.

His office had the drab colours, the stripped-down, bare-essentials look of military installations everywhere.

General Chellak himself was a tired-looking middle-aged man with a neat military moustache. He was a career soldier, conscientious rather than inspired. He had the depressed, defeated look of a man who has been grappling with a hopeless task for far too long. (Like his men, Chellak wore simple workaday combat uniform, with only his yellow shoulder-patches to indicate high rank.)

There was a brisk rap on the door, and Chellak looked up from his never-ending duty-rosters. 'Yes?' Major Salateen, his aide-de-camp, marched into the room.

With a flicker of mild irritation, Chellak saw that Salateen looked as fresh and alert as always, uniform and accessories gleaming, fair hair brushed neatly back. Wryly Chellak told himself he was being unfair. Salateen was an invaluable right-hand man, hard-working and efficient. Even the ordeal of capture by the enemy hadn't worried him – he had simply escaped and returned more tireless and determined than ever.

Major Salateen saluted. 'Message from Captain Rones, sir. His men have just captured two gun-runners.'

Chellak rose and went over to the map of the cave systems that took up most of one wall. 'Good, good! That's excellent. Well done, Rones, eh?' He tapped one of the coloured pins that studded the map. 'He's B group, I think?'

'Yes, sir.'

'Excellent!' repeated Chellak. 'About time we had some success, eh? Did they resist?'

'Apparently not, sir. The patrol also captured an arms dump – gas weapons.'

Chellak swung round alarmed. 'Gas?'

Salateen nodded. 'Captain Rones suspects there may be more gun-runners in the area. He wants to know if he should stay in place, set up an ambush.'

'I think it's more important we should see these captured weapons, Major Salateen.'

'Very good, sir.'

Worriedly, Chellak stroked his moustache. 'If Sharaz Jek gets his hands on gas weapons we shall be in the devil of a stew.'

'We have gas suits in the stores, General.'

'Bad design, always said so. A few hours in one of

those things and you start to cook. Still, better have 'em checked, ready for issue.'

'It's already being done, sir.'

Again, that remorseless efficiency.

Chellak forced a smile. 'Ahead of me as usual, eh, Salateen? Now, what about these prisoners?'

In his penthouse office high above the towering super-city of Androzani, capital of Androzani Major, Trau Morgus, Chairman of the Sirius Conglomerate, was studying the readout screen on a desk computer, his thin, pinched features frozen in an expression of distaste. Morgus was a middle-aged middle-sized man, wearing the rich bronze garments that denoted the highest executive rank. His hair was scraped back, drawn into the neat pigtail of Androzanian aristocracy.

He touched a desk control. The door to his suite slid silently open, revealing a tall, fair-haired woman in a rich blue gown. Her shining blonde hair was brushed into a gleaming cap, and her face wore the same air of cold efficiency as Morgus's own. Long glittering earrings added the only touch of femininity. 'Yes, sir?'

Without looking up, Morgus said, 'Krau Timmin, copper output has risen thirteen per cent. That should not have occurred.' Even when he was angry, Morgus's voice seldom rose above a whisper.

Defensively Timmin said, 'Head of Minerals did send out a limiting order last month, sir.'

'Too little, too late! Tell him he is to fly out

15

immediately to Northcawl Mine. I want a feasibility study on the possibility of closure.'

'Yes, sir.'

'That is all, Krau Timmin.'

To his surprise, Timmin stayed where she was. Morgus looked up. 'Well?'

'There is a message from General Chellak, sir.'

'Yes?'

'The General wishes to inform you that his men have captured two gun-runners, and intercepted an arms delivery to the android rebels.'

Morgus was silent for a moment. He seemed to take little pleasure in the news, thought Timmin. But then, Morgus showed few emotions of any kind.

'Ah,' said Morgus at last. 'Taken two gun-runners alive, eh? Get me Chellak on vision.'

'Yes, sir.' Timmin left.

Morgus sat staring into space. Slowly a muscle beneath his eye began to twitch. 'Spineless cretins!'

From his hiding place behind the rocks, Stotz watched the soldiers carrying away the arms. He scowled. In the hands of the Army those guns meant danger, to him and to his employer. He crawled back to his men who were crouched down further back.

'They're starting to move the stuff out. If we work our way round we can cut them off.'

'How many?' asked Krelper nervously.

'Ten, maybe a dozen. We can handle them. Come on lads, let's fumigate some squaddies!'

They moved away.

Chellak looked unhappily at the casualty report on his desk. It reported the death of Trooper Boze, at the hands, or rather the fangs and claws, of the magma beast that lurked in the lower levels.

He looked unhappily up at Salateen. 'There was a whole survey team charting Blue Level. Didn't anyone see anything?'

'Apparently not, sir. They heard Trooper Boze cry out and they ran back but, well, it was like the others. The thing hadn't left much of him.'

Chellak threw down the report. 'That's five men now. Always on Blue Level. If we had the time and the manpower, I'd send a squad down there to find and destroy it.'

Salateen made one of his rare jokes. 'It'd make a nice trophy for the mess, sir!'

The door opened, and a soldier entered and saluted. He stepped aside to make way for two more soldiers, pushing the Doctor and Peri before them.

The Doctor looked round the room, taking in the drab military grey of the walls and the equipment, the shabby, worn air of a place designed for temporary use that has somehow become permanent. He studied Chellak too. A soldier under pressure, thought the Doctor. Never the easiest type to deal with.

Chellak looked at the two prisoners and indicated the area before his desk. 'Stand here.'

17

'Couldn't we have a chair?' asked the Doctor politely. 'It's been rather a strenuous day.'

At a nod from Chellak, the troopers shoved the Doctor and Peri forwards.

'You will stand there until I have finished with you,' said Chellak coldly. 'And when you address me, you will call me "sir".'

'And may I ask you who you are – *sir*?'

'I am General Chellak, Commander of all Federal Forces on Androzani Minor.'

The Doctor couldn't resist mocking the pomposity of this announcement. 'Well done – sir! I suppose you started in the ranks?'

Chellak stared coldly at him. 'Under Emergency Regulations, anyone caught supplying arms to the android rebels faces summary execution.'

'But we weren't supplying arms,' protested Peri. 'We were – well, we just found them there . . .'

'. . . *sir*,' completed the Doctor.

'However,' Chellak continued, 'If you co-operate, I am prepared to extend clemency. If you do not co-operate, you will be shot. Is that clear?'

The Doctor said, 'You couldn't have put it more plainly. Exactly how do we co-operate?'

'. . . *sir*,' reminded Peri in turn.

'Thank you, Peri,' said the Doctor politely. 'How do we co-operate, *sir*?'

'Do not provoke me,' shouted Chellak.

Suddenly the Doctor decided that the joke had gone far enough. 'Sorry.'

'I want to know your names, and the names of all

18

your confederates. I want full details of all armaments deliveries, where and how they are brought in. I want to know who supplies you with the arms back on Major. And what your communications arrangements are with Sharaz Jek.'

'Well, I'm generally known as the Doctor, and my young friend here is called Perpugilliam Brown – Peri for short.'

'Go on.'

'I'm afraid that's it! That's all we can tell you!'

'Don't waste my time!'

'If we could just sit down and talk about this little misunderstanding in a civilised manner,' pleaded the Doctor. 'My young friend here has been suffering from pains in her legs. You can see for yourself, she's suffering from some form of urticaria . . .'

He indicated a spreading rash on Peri's legs.

'Silence,' snapped Chellak.

The Doctor ignored him. 'Come to that, I don't feel too well myself.'

There was a bleep from the com-set on Chellak's desk. 'Yes?'

'Signal for you, sir. Trau Morgus is on vid. He wants to speak to you immediately, General.'

Chellak frowned. 'Very well, I'll take it.' He nodded towards the door. 'Take them away.'

As the soldiers herded them out, Peri turned to the Doctor and said sadly, 'I don't think he likes us very much.'

The soldiers bustled them away.

* * *

19

Chairman Morgus was in top-secret conference with a thin, sharp-faced man wrapped in a black cloak. 'Now remember, I want the operation at Northcawl completed by the morning.'

The stranger nodded silently.

Morgus touched a desk-button and a section of wall slid back, revealing a lift. 'Take my private lift, and make sure you're not seen on the way out.'

'Yes, Trau Morgus,' said the thin man softly.

He stepped into the lift, and the door slid closed behind him.

Morgus touched a control and his picture-window darkened and became a vid-screen. Chellak's features appeared.

Without preliminary, Morgus snapped, 'These captured gun-runners . . . what information have you obtained?'

'Nothing as yet, sir. Only their names.'

'And what are their names?'

'The man calls himself the Doctor, and the girl's name is Peri.'

'A girl?' said Morgus curiously. 'Bring them to the screen.'

General Chellak gave an order to someone out of view. He turned back to Morgus. 'I've only just begun the interrogation. I hope to get enough out of these two to round up the rest of the gang.'

'I hope so too, General Chellak, for your sake. Your operation so far has been a dismal failure.'

Chellak's face darkened with anger. 'With respect, sir, I don't believe you understand the difficulty of conditions here – '

Morgus interrupted him. 'All I understand is this – you are supposed to be trained soldiers, yet one renegade and a handful of mindless androids have been dancing rings round you for six months.'

'May I remind you, Trau Morgus, we captured the spectrox refinery on our very first assault.'

'And allowed Sharaz Jek to spirit away the entire stock-pile from under your very nose. I warn you, General Chellak, people here are not prepared to suffer your blundering for much longer . . .'

In his workshop deep beneath the cave system, Sharaz Jek, the subject of this discussion, was sitting before a bank of video screens. One screen showed Chellak, the other Morgus, and the sound of their wrangling came over quite clearly.

It seemed to be giving Sharaz Jek considerable pleasure, if one could judge by the gleam of interest in his eyes. The rest of Sharaz Jek's face was concealed by a skin-tight leather mask. He leaned forward, following the discussion.

Chellak was saying angrily, 'I'm sorry, Trau Morgus, but I simply will not accept such criticism from a civilian, however highly placed . . .'

Suddenly two figures appeared on Chellak's screen, a slender fair-haired man and a dark-haired girl.

'Tempers getting a little frayed, are they?' said the man cheerfully.

Morgus said, 'I take it you are the one who calls himself the Doctor? I am Morgus, Chief Director of the Sirius Conglomerate.'

'I know – and we have to address you as "sir".'

Their discussion held no interest for Sharaz Jek. He touched a control and suddenly Peri's face alone filled the screen.

Sharaz Jek leaned forward eagerly, caressing the face on the screen with a black-gloved hand.

Morgus stared coldly at the two figures on his vidscreen. 'Better if you do not address me at all,' he was saying. 'I merely wished to inspect you, to see the kind of creatures capable of betraying the golden vision of our glorious pioneers.' His face twisted with distaste. 'Already I feel contaminated. Get rid of them.'

Soldiers hustled the Doctor and Peri away, and Chellak took their place on the screen.

'You have done well, General Chellak,' said Morgus smoothly. 'I am sorry if my earlier remarks appeared intemperate. It is just that I long to stand shoulder-to-shoulder with you in the struggle. All right-thinking citizens must feel the same.' Morgus paused. 'And so to boost morale, I want your two captives executed immediately.'

'Executed? But I've already told them their lives will be spared if they collaborate.'

Morgus shook his head. 'No. No collaboration, General, no deals with traitors. The public will not stand for it.'

'If we shoot them out of hand, we lose the chance of getting valuable information out of them – '

'That may be true, but it is not of prime importance. These people are the lowest type of human being. One has only to look at them to realise the full extent of their depravity. Get rid of them, General, and we shall all feel a lot better.' Morgus's voice hardened. 'The prisoners are to be executed – immediately!'

3

The Execution

Stotz and his band of gun-runners had chosen their position very carefully. They were hidden behind a jumble of loose boulders at the point where the cave system emerged into one of the ravines called narrows.

They had a longish wait, but eventually their patience was rewarded. The patrol of Federal troops appeared, moving slowly, burdened with the crates.

'Here they come,' whispered Stotz. 'Masks.'

The gun-runners pulled up the masks that hung around their necks.

As the troopers emerged into daylight they stopped for a moment, putting down the crates, stretching their aching backs, mopping their brows and grumbling to each other. It was a natural enough reaction, and it was exactly what Stotz had been counting on. 'Now!'

Slipping a gas-grenade from his cross-belt, Stotz tossed it towards the unsuspecting patrol.

At the sight of the red cylinder arcing towards

them the troopers reacted instantly, grabbing for their weapons.

The grenade exploded at their feet with a soft plop, and greasy yellow fumes swirled through the ravine.

As the soldiers staggered back choking there came another grenade and then another. Soon the ravine was filled with swirling clouds of gas.

The soldiers got off one or two wild shots, but one by one they choked and fell. A few minutes later their scattered bodies were strewn across the floor of the ravine.

Krelper tapped Stotz on the arm and gave a triumphant thumbs-up sign. Stotz grinned wolfishly, and signalled his men to move forwards.

The Doctor and Peri meanwhile were arguing for their lives, though with very little success.

Calmly and logically the Doctor had pointed out all the facts in his own and Peri's favour. Their alien appearance and manner of dress – whatever they were, they clearly weren't citizens of Androzani Major. The fact that they were unarmed, and had made no attempt to escape or to resist. Surely, the Doctor pointed out, the two of them made a most unlikely pair of gun-runners.

General Chellak listened to the Doctor's arguments with surprising patience, even seemed to be influenced by them. But finally he shook his head and said gloomily, 'I'm afraid you're wasting your time, Doctor. You heard Morgus. He wants you executed.'

Peri just couldn't take it in. 'But that's barbaric!'

The Doctor tried an appeal to Chellak's military pride. 'You take orders from a civilian? Weren't you just telling us *you* command the Federal forces here?'

'I could appeal the order, I suppose, but it would be useless. Morgus has the Praesidium in his pocket.'

The Doctor began to despair. 'We're quite innocent, you know. This is all a mistake.'

'I think I'm beginning to believe you, Doctor. But in time of war sometimes the innocent die too.'

'Is that all you're going to say?' Peri burst out. 'We're going to be killed – '

She was interrupted by the entrance of Major Salateen. 'A message from Captain Rones, sir. His men are under gas attack.'

Chellak jumped up. 'Where?'

'They were ambushed – in the narrows. The message broke off, sir . . .'

'That's barely six hundred metres from here. Muster HQ Platoon.'

'They're falling in now, sir. Shall I take them out?'

'No, I will. Put these two in the detention cells, and get them ready for execution.'

Chellak turned and hurried away.

Salateen looked curiously at the two victims. 'You have heard of death under the red cloth, Doctor?'

'I'm afraid not.'

'It is a military procedure. After death, your

bodies will be taken to the Field Cremation Unit. Your ashes will be wrapped in the red cloth of execution and disposed of as you direct.'

'It doesn't sound any more enticing than any other form of death,' said the Doctor wearily.

Major Salateen beckoned to the guards at the door. 'Place these two in detention.'

The guards took the Doctor and Peri away.

Morgus sat at his enormous desk, gazing out of his picture-window at the mist-shrouded towers of Androzani City. 'I think I made the right decision. I only wish the execution could be made public.'

'That isn't possible, sir,' said Krau Timmin regretfully.

'I know. But think of the prestige it would bring the Conglomerate.' He swung round and looked sharply at her. 'To witness the punishment of wrongdoers is excellent moral reinforcement, do you not agree?'

'Oh, yes indeed, sir!' Krau Timmin always agreed with everything her employer said, outwardly at least. Her private thoughts she kept very much to herself. 'The President is coming to see you at five, sir.'

'Ah yes. Take ten centilitres of spectrox from my private stock. Even His Excellency cannot expect more than ten centilitres in these difficult times.'

Krau Timmin made rapid notes on the miniaturised computer-terminal that was always in her hand, and hurried away.

Morgus resumed his thoughtful staring out of the window.

By now the gas had cleared in the narrows. Stotz and his gun-runners were moving amongst the bodies of the soldiers recovering the captured crates of weapons.

There had been a brief but vicious argument about their disposition. Krelper had been in favour of repossessing the weapons and making another attempt to make contact with the elusive Sharaz Jek.

Stotz however had pointed out that very soon the caves would be swarming with yet more Federal troops. The captain of the ambushed patrol had got some kind of message out, and Chellak would certainly send more soldiers to investigate. If the gun-runners tried to move about the caves burdened by the arms crates, their capture and summary execution was certain. With the arms abandoned they could travel light and make a quick getaway. Even if they were captured it would be a lot harder to prove anything against them, with the evidence destroyed.

As usual, Stotz had had his way. At this point the narrows bordered a deep gully, an apparently bottomless ravine which disappeared into the depths of the planet.

The gun-runners were dragging the weapon crates towards it, and pitching them over the edge, one by one. 'Come on,' yelled Stotz. 'Move it!'

As the last crate tumbled over, Stotz alerted. Listening like a hunted animal, he could hear the faint jingle of equipment, the sound of booted feet on rock. 'Soldiers! Come on, hurry!'

The gun-runners fled, disappearing round a bend in the narrows.

Seconds later, General Chellak appeared with his patrol. For a moment he stood gazing in horror at the scattered corpses. He checked a wrist-gauge then slowly removed his protective mask.

He moved amongst the scattered bodies, checking them one by one. 'Dead, every last man,' he said bleakly. 'They killed the whole patrol.' He turned to his second-in-command. 'Check that the other areas are free of gas – and get a stretcher party down here.'

The trooper saluted and moved away.

General Chellak stood staring down at the dead bodies of his men.

The cell into which the Doctor and Peri were thrust was just that, a cell. A square metal box without even a bunk or a chair, with the usual eye-grille set into the heavy door.

The Doctor and Peri were sitting on the floor, backs to the wall, arms hugging their knees.

'There was something very funny about that Major Salateen,' said the Doctor broodingly.

Peri recalled her impressions of the cold-faced, impassively handsome young Major. 'There was? He didn't make me laugh.'

The Doctor seemed to be pursuing some train of thought. 'And Chellak said they were fighting *android* rebels . . .'

'Who cares who they're fighting? We seem to be the fall guys.'

'Yes . . . do try to speak English, Peri.'

'Doctor, we've got about an hour to live. That Morgus wants us dead.'

'That's another odd thing,' said the Doctor thoughtfully. 'He had us paraded up and down in front of him and then he seemed to lose all interest. I found that rather insulting.'

'I can take insults,' said Peri dismissively. 'I just don't want to be shot. Doctor, what are we going to do?'

'I've really no idea. I'm sorry I got you into this, Peri.'

'It's all right. It was my fault as much as yours.'

The Doctor shook his head. 'No, I should never have followed those tracks. Curiosity has always been my downfall. How's your rash, by the way?'

Peri looked at her legs. 'I seem to be coming out in blisters now.'

The Doctor studied his own hands, and pushed back his sleeves to look at his wrists and arms. 'Me too. That fungus must have had some very toxic properties.'

Peri made a brave attempt at a black joke. 'Well, I don't suppose we'll die of it – not within the next hour anyway.'

The Doctor rose and peered through the grille in

the cell door. It looked out onto a quite sizeable cave, a kind of natural hall. In the centre of this open space a squad of soldiers were fitting heavy wooden posts into sockets carved in the rock floor. The posts were big and heavy, made of scarred and pitted wood, with leather straps dangling from the sides. Execution posts, thought the Doctor.

'What can you see?' asked Peri. 'Anything interesting?'

The Doctor turned away from the door. 'No, no,' he said hastily, 'everything's very quiet. It's like a graveyard out there.'

He caught Peri's gaze, and immediately wished that he'd chosen some other image.

In his underground workshop, the masked figure of Sharaz Jek was crouched over a communications console. He was studying a video recording of the interview between the Doctor and Peri and Morgus, running it through the machine, over and over again.

As he watched, his black-gloved hands were busy on a neighbouring scanner-console, feeding graph-lines, contours, measurements and a flood of other data into its memory banks.

When he was satisfied, he unplugged the scanner, moved across the workshop and plugged the scanner into a long, coffin-shaped container filled with a bubbling fluid, so thick and viscous as to be almost solid.

The black-gloved hand reached out and pulled a

lever. Sharaz Jek returned to his communications console. 'Sharaz Jek calling Base Defence Group. Numbers Four and Nine report to me immediately.'

He operated more controls, and somewhere in General Chellak's HQ a tiny panel slid back high in the rock wall, revealing a telescopic camera lens.

On one of Sharaz Jek's screens a picture appeared, showing a file of soldiers bearing dead bodies on stretchers. The black-clad figure chuckled hoarsely. 'Stotz must have had a good day . . .'

The Doctor was pacing up and down the detention cell. 'That fellow Morgus said spectrox was the most valuable stuff in the universe. I wonder why? What can it be?'

'I thought you knew everything, Doctor.'

'Ah, well, not quite. It's going to worry me until I find out what it is!'

Peri had been looking through the grille. She turned away from the door. 'I don't think you'll have to worry long, Doctor. They seem to be about ready for us.'

The Doctor went to look.

The posts were firmly in place now, and a squad of soldiers was falling in under the orders of an officer.

Absorbed in the sinister scene, neither the Doctor nor Peri noticed that behind them in the cell a hidden panel was slowly sliding open . . .

* * *

Morgus held out a small silver phial and the President reached for it, trying not to appear too eager. 'My dear Morgus, I can't thank you enough.'

The President was a tall, silver-haired man in the cloth of gold worn only by those of the highest rank. Like many politicians he was handsome in a rather actorish way. The tanned, youthful features contrasted with the mane of silver-grey hair.

Morgus bowed deeply, striving to conceal the contempt he felt for this posturing jack-in-office. 'My pleasure, Trau President. How much do you take?'

'My apothecary recommends a dose of zero point three centilitres a day.' The President smiled confidentially. 'I've been without for three weeks now, and between you and me, I was beginning to feel my age.'

'Spectrox is indeed a wonderful restorative.'

'The greatest boon ever bestowed on humanity. After all, it offers us at least twice the normal lifespan.'

The President preened himself brushing back the silvery hair. 'Would you ever think I was eighty-four?'

'Fifty at the most,' said Morgus, and he was speaking the truth.

This was the secret of spectrox, the reason for its extraordinary value. It gave, if not immortality, the next best thing, a prolonged and healthy middle age. It enabled men like the President to lead active, enjoyable lives, remaining in office when they might otherwise have been in wheelchairs or in hospital beds waiting for death.

Spectrox could be produced only in relatively small quantities, and it was so costly that only those of the highest rank and the greatest wealth could be assured of regular supplies. Men like the President, and Morgus himself, together with a select group of politicans and business tycoons of Androzani Major.

A small, a very small amount was exported to similarly powerful figures on the rest of the Five Planets. Spectrox had been in production for some years now, long enough for its effect to be seen and its fame to spread. It had always been enormously expensive, but the rebellion on Androzani Minor and the consequent shortage of supply had driven the price higher still.

The President said impressively, 'This war *must* be brought to a conclusion soon, Morgus. One way or another.'

'There is only one honourable way, sir,' said Morgus quickly. 'Sharaz Jek must be crushed.'

'Of course. But our forces are making such poor progress, and meanwhile there is a clamour for the supplies of spectrox to be resumed. It is understandable.'

'That clamour is the razor's edge that Sharaz Jek is holding to our throats. We cannot accede to criminal blackmail!'

The President spread his hands in a politician's gesture. 'My dear Morgus, personally speaking I agree entirely. But we in the Praesidium are forced to look at the matter from a different viewpoint.'

'Patriotism is the only viewpoint.'

The President rose and moved to look out of the window. 'A businessman's patriotism may be different to that of a politician. I am forced to take account of the mood of the Praesidium, of people of influence. That mood is becoming ugly.' He swung round upon Morgus. 'Whereas you, my dear Morgus, need only take account of your balance sheets – which, since the market value of spectrox has risen so astronomically, must now look even healthier than they did at the start of the conflict!'

Morgus was quick to defend himself. 'My conglomerate is contributing handsomely towards the cost of operations on Androzani Minor.'

'Yes indeed, and the Praesidium is duly grateful. But as your congromerate owns that planet, such a contribution is, perhaps, no more than might be expected.'

Morgus decided it was time to confront the issue. 'Trau President, am I to understand that the Praesidium is considering ending the war – offering Sharaz Jek some kind of armistice?'

The President chose his words carefully. 'Not – immediately. However, if the military stalemate continues . . .' He shrugged. 'The Praesidium wants its spectrox, Morgus.'

The door opened and Krau Timmin appeared.

Morgus looked up impatiently at her. 'Yes, what is it?'

'It is time for the executions, sir.'

General Chellak stood watching grim-faced as the firing squad formed a line before the execution stakes, and ordered arms. Nervously he fiddled with the ceremonial sword at his side. He nodded to Salateen who marched up to the cell.

The door was unlocked and Salateen went inside. The Doctor and Peri stood side by side, looking towards him, their faces unnaturally calm. They were already wearing the long hooded red cloaks that had been brought to them a short time before.

'Are you ready?' asked Salateen.

The Doctor and Peri nodded.

In his workshop, Sharaz Jek leaned forwards in fascination, watching as the Doctor and Peri were led to the execution stakes and strapped into place.

He threw back his weirdly-masked head and laughed.

Morgus, the President and Krau Timmin stood watching the scene on the screen that had appeared on the picture-window.

The President snorted. 'They wear the red cloth. Disgraceful!'

'It is a military execution,' Morgus said calmly.

The President snorted. 'In my day we'd have given filthy little swine like that a bullet in the back of the head. The red cloth was for soldiers!'

* * *

By now the Doctor and Peri were strapped firmly on the stakes.

General Chellak stepped forward. 'Do you have any last declaration?'

'Nothing special,' said the Doctor, still speaking with that same unnatural calm. 'We have had no trial. We have had no opportunity to defend ourselves. In short, this is a mockery of justice.' So calm was the Doctor's voice that he might have been discussing an abstract point of law, something that didn't affect him personally at all.

Chellak moved on to Peri. 'Do you have any last declaration?'

Peri was staring impassively ahead of her. 'Just get on with it.' Like the Doctor's, her voice was flat and calm.

Chellak nodded to the sergeant in charge of the firing squad. He pulled the floppy hoods forward so that they covered the Doctor's and Peri's faces.

Chellak drew his sword, and held it high.

'Firing squad – firing position!'

The squad raised the stubby machine-pistols.

'Take aim!'

Three of the machine-pistols converged on the Doctor, the other three on Peri.

'Fire!'

The sword swept down.

The two bound and red-cloaked figures at the stakes jerked and twisted under the impact of a hail of bullets.

4

Sharaz Jek

Morgus looked thoughtfully at his vid-screen. It showed a close-up of two red-cloaked figures slumped forwards at the execution-posts, held upright only by the restraining straps.

He flicked off the screen and turned politely to the President. 'Whatever his defects as a commander, one must admit that Chellak brings a certain style to these things, does he not?'

'Indeed,' said the President, with equal formality. 'Though I feel the decision to execute may have been precipitate. Some useful information might have been extracted from them.'

'They were merely pawns, Excellency, ignorant handlers of smuggled goods. The slums of the city are full of such unemployed riff-raff.'

'Most of them are unemployed, Trau Morgus, because you have closed so many of your manufacturing plants. It has caused great unrest.'

'The matter is easily settled, Excellency. All those without valid employment cards should be sent off to the Eastern labour camps.'

'Yes, that might be made to seem morally justifiable. 'I'll put your interesting suggestion to the Praesidium tomorrow.'

The President rose and began moving towards the door.

Morgus hurried to open it for him. 'Naturally, Excellency, should any special funding be required, my conglomerate would be happy to assist.'

'Most generous.' The President paused in the doorway as if struck by a sudden thought. 'Of course, Trau Morgus, the irony is, that while you've been closing plants here in the West, you've been building them in the East. So, if the unemployed were to be sent to the Eastern labour camps, a great many of them would still be working for you, only this time without payment.'

'You know, I hadn't thought of that,' said Morgus, with an air of mild surprise.

The President smiled. 'Of course you hadn't.' With a nod of farewell, he strolled from the office.

Morgus returned to his desk, and resumed his brooding survey of the towers of Androzani City. He had much to consider.

The Doctor and Peri had been not unnaturally surprised when a panel in their cell wall had slid open, and two replicas of themselves had emerged. The replicas had been followed by two more androids, human in form but faceless. Instead of a human head there was only a gleaming white egg with one huge eye.

39

The two replicas had taken the hooded red robes from the Doctor and Peri and put them on, while the other androids indicated that they should follow them back through the panel.

The Doctor and Peri had thought it wise to obey. For one thing the androids were armed with machine-pistols, much like those carried by the soldiers. More important, whatever alternative they were offering, it was surely better than summary execution.

The androids led them along a secret passage that emerged into one of the cave galleries.

There had followed a longish journey, first through the narrows, and then down into caves several levels lower. They had come at last to a concealed door in the rock-face. The androids opened it, and urged them forwards.

They found themselves in an underground base, like a more primitive version of General Chellak's HQ. Rooms and corridors were formed from the natural rock, though they showed signs of having been shaped and enlarged. It was a grim, gloomy place, like the underground lair of some savage beast.

The androids led them along the corridors and into a long, thin, irregularly-shaped room that appeared to be a combined laboratory, workshop and communications centre, with work benches and instrument consoles contrasting strangely with the grim rock walls.

An extraordinary figure swung round from a

console to confront them. It was clad from head to foot in a skin-tight one-piece garment made from some shiny black material. The head was completely covered by a close-fitting mask, with slits for eyes and mouth. The face-part of the mask was parti-coloured, black and white. The lower right half of the apparition's face was black, the upper half white; on the other side of the face the pattern was more or less reversed. The total effect, thought the Doctor, was that of an evil and demented harlequin. He bowed. 'Sharaz Jek, I presume?'

Glittering eyes surveyed them through the mask-slits. 'What remains of him.' The voice was a hoarse, rasping whisper. 'Sit down, you must be tired.'

Sharaz Jek glided forwards, staring at Peri with evident fascination. A black-gloved hand took her by the arm and guided her to a bench.

Terrified, Peri sat.

The Doctor sank down beside her. 'Thank you.'

Sharaz Jek loomed over them, studying them through the mask-slits with glittering eyes.

General Chellak straightened up. 'Androids!'

However human androids can be made to appear on the outside, their inner workings are drastically different. When the bullet-shattered bodies revealed not blood but circuitry, Ensign Cass, the officer in charge of the disposal squad, had summoned Chellak in some alarm.

Chellak studied the bodies unbelievingly. 'An-

41

droids,' he said again. 'But so lifelike. I could have sworn they were human.'

'Sharaz Jek is improving,' said Salateen grimly.

'And these are his creatures. Is he using androids now for gun-running, do you think?'

'He must be, sir. And unlike his soldiers, the gun-runner androids would have to pass for human, so they could operate back on Major.' Salateen gestured towards the two shattered android bodies. 'Presumably that's why he's perfected them to this extent.'

Chellak stroked his moustache. 'Yes, of course . . . You know, the man must be a genius in his way.'

'Shall you inform the Praesidium of what has happened?'

Chellak stared agitatedly at him. 'How can I? If it ever got out that I'd solemnly executed two androids under the red cloth, I'd be the laughing stock of the Army, the butt of a thousand jokes. I'd be finished. It mustn't get out!'

Major Salateen's face was impassive. 'There is no reason why it should, sir. Apart from ourselves only Ensign Cass is aware of what has happened.'

'Cass? Is he reliable?'

'He could be sent on a deep-penetration mission, sir. Very few return.'

Sharaz Jek was interrogating his captives.

'Then if you are not from Androzani Major, where are you from – Earth?'

'Yes,' said Peri.

'No,' said the Doctor.

Peri corrected herself. 'That is, not exactly.'

'We travel a lot,' explained the Doctor.

'Interesting. We shall have much to talk about. I was a doctor myself before the study of androids took over my life.'

'Oh, really?' said the Doctor politely. 'Well, it would be nice to stay and chat a bit longer, but we really must be going, now we've rested. If you'll just point us towards the surface . . .'

The Doctor didn't really expect this approach to work, and it didn't.

'No, Doctor,' whispered Sharaz Jek. 'You must stay here now.

'Stay here? For how long?' asked Peri nervously.

Sharaz Jek moved closer, leaning over her. It was clear that his words were addressed to her alone. 'I shall make you quite comfortable. After a few years, you will be quite content, living here with me.'

A black-gloved hand caressed Peri's shoulder. 'Yes,' whispered Sharaz Jek. 'Quite content . . .'

The gun-runners had set up camp in a hollow of the sand dunes, just outside the caves. Now they were waiting, and the inactivity was getting on their nerves. They stood in a little group, muttering uneasily.

Only Stotz, the leader, seemed calm and relaxed. He was dozing peacefully a little apart from his men, head pillowed on his back-pack.

Krelper detached himself from the group and walked over to him. He stopped, staring down at his leader's prone body.

'Stotzy, the guys aren't taking no more of this.'

Stotz didn't even open his eyes. 'No more of what?'

'This hanging about, waiting to make contact. We want paying, and we want out.'

Stotz got slowly to his feet. He yawned and stretched. 'Do you now?'

Krelper nodded. 'According to contract, Stotzy.'

'According to contract, eh? Contract says you get paid back on Major.'

'A two-day job, you said.'

Krelper broke off choking, as Stotz's hand grabbed him suddenly by the windpipe.

'A two-day job, I said – if we were lucky. But we weren't lucky – were we, Krelper?' Suddenly there was a long bayonet-like knife in Stotz's other hand. 'And your luck runs out right now!'

Krelper wrenched himself free, and backed nervously away. 'Take it easy, Stotzy,' he gasped. 'Take it easy!'

Stotz stalked towards him. 'You guys have only got one option. You can either stick with me, or you can stay here forever!' He brandished the knife.

Krelper backed nervously towards the ravine. 'Come on, now, cut it out, Stotzy . . .'

'The only thing I'm cutting out is your black heart.'

Stotz sprang forward, bearing Krelper to the

44

ground, so that his head jutted out over the edge of the ravine, holding him there with the knife at his throat.

'No, no,' pleaded Krelper. 'For pity's sake,' Stotz groped in a pocket with his free hand and produced a small black capsule. 'The Boss gave me this. Death in ten seconds, he said. Let's see if he's right!'

'No,' screamed Krelper. 'No, no . . .'

Suddenly Stotz thrust the capsule into Krelper's open mouth, and then jammed the mouth shut with a hand under the jaw.

'Come on, Krelper, bite! Bite! Bite! Bite!'

Krelper struggled furiously, twisting his head away, trying desperately not to crush the capsule.

Stotz held him a moment longer, and then released him.

Krelper scrambled to his feet, retching, spitting the capsule out into the sand.

'Next time it'll be for real,' said Stotz. He went back to his back-pack, stretched out and began to doze.

The gleaming eye in the blank white face of the android guard followed Peri to and fro as she stamped awkwardly about the workshop.

The Doctor, who had been dozing uneasily on one of the benches, opened his eyes. 'What's the matter, Peri?'

'Cramp,' said Peri briefly, and went on stamping.

'Try touching your toes.'

Peri obeyed.

'That's it,' encouraged the Doctor. 'And again!'

Sharaz Jek appeared in the doorway. 'Working up an appetite? Salateen will be bringing your food shortly.'

Peri stared at him. 'Major Salateen? Have you captured him too?'

'Quite some time ago, my dear.'

'But we saw him – he was at HQ.'

'I imagine the Salateen we saw was an android,' said the Doctor gently. 'The real Salateen is a prisoner here, like us.' He turned to Sharaz Jek. 'We haven't met him yet. Where is he chained up?'

Sharaz Jek smiled – or at least, the lips beneath the mouth-slit seemed to twitch. 'Chains are unnecessary here, Doctor, as you will discover!'

Sharaz Jek seemed fascinated by Peri. He moved towards her, as if drawn by some magnetic attraction, and stood gazing down at her.

Peri stared defiantly up at him. 'Why are you keeping us here?'

'Oh, my exquisite child,' whispered Sharaz Jek. 'How could I ever let you go? The sight of beauty is so important to me.' He glanced briefly at the Doctor. 'Not to mention the stimulus of a mind nearly equal to my own.'

The Doctor gave him an indignant look. 'Thank you!'

The hoarse voice went on, whispering in Peri's ear. 'I have missed so much of life, these last lonely years. Now your arrival has changed all that. We shall become the best of friends.'

The Doctor raised his voice challengingly. 'What do you say, Peri? We can go on nature walks in the caves, have picnics and jolly evenings round the camp fire.'

Sharaz Jek swung round menacingly. 'Do not mock me, Doctor. Beauty I must have – but you are dispensable.'

The Doctor bowed mockingly. 'Thank you,' he said again.

Sharaz Jek stalked towards him, staring down into the Doctor's face. The Doctor met his gaze unflinchingly.

'You have the mouth of a prattling jackanapes,' said Sharaz Jek thoughtfully. 'Yet your eyes tell a different story.' He turned indifferently away. 'No matter. I shall break you to my will – and if I cannot break you, then I shall kill you.' He turned back to Peri. 'But you, my child, will live forever.'

Peri stared at him. 'Nobody lives forever.'

'He means it will seem like forever,' said the Doctor irrepressibly.

'Spectrox is the key to eternal life, holding at bay the ravages of time,' whispered Sharaz Jek huskily. 'The flower of your beauty will be as permanent as a precious jewel untarnished by the passing years.'

'Well, well, well,' said the Doctor. 'Now we know why spectrox is the most valuable substance in the universe.'

'It is indeed,' croaked Sharaz Jek. 'And it is mine – all of it!'

'Until the Army take it away from you,' said the Doctor matter-of-factly.

'That possibility does not exist, Doctor. I know every move they make.'

Peri did her best to support the Doctor. 'Knowing what the Army's doing and stopping them from doing it, are two different things.'

'Exactly,' said the Doctor. 'General Chellak is working to a plan. I've seen his operations board.'

'Have you, Doctor?' sneered Sharaz Jek. 'Then see mine!' He strode over to a console and stabbed at controls. Immediately a computer map lit up, showing a cross-section of the labyrinthine cave systems, shaded in different colours.

The Doctor studied the map eagerly, committing it to memory as he did so. 'What's this green area here?'

'That is the area held by the Army.'

'So, they've already sealed you off to the north?'

'Already?' Sharaz Jek laughed mockingly. 'To get that far has taken Chellak six months, and it has cost him hundreds of casualties. Computing that same rate of advance as standard, it will be another five years before I am seriously threatened!'

'Perhaps so. But what's five years when you're having a good war?'

Sharaz Jek's voice was shaking with anger. 'The people of Androzani Major will not wait five years for their spectrox, Doctor. Long before that, they

48

will rise in protest, and the Praesidium will be forced to agree to my terms.'

'And what are your terms?' asked Peri.

The weirdly masked face stared into her own. 'They can have the spectrox they want when I have the head of Morgus, here at my feet.' The voice rose to a screech. 'I want the head of that perfidious, treacherous degenerate brought to me here, congealed in its own evil blood . . .'

Shaking with rage, Sharaz Jek swung round and lurched from the workshop.

5

The Escape

Morgus looked up as Krau Timmin came into his office. 'What is it?'

'The Northcawl copper mine, sir. There's been a disaster. I thought you should know.'

'What kind of disaster?'

'An explosion, Trau Morgus, early this morning. The mine has been completely destroyed.'

Morgus shook his head regretfully. 'Tut, tut, how sad.' There was only the most perfunctory concern in the flat voice. 'However, the loss of Northcawl eliminates our little problem of over-production. The news should also raise the market price of copper.'

'Undoubtedly, sir,' said Krau Timmin deferentially.

Morgus smiled thinly. 'As they used to say on Earth, every cloud has a strontium lining, eh, Krau Timmin?'

'Yes, sir. Yes, indeed.'

'As a mark of respect to our late executives, I want every employee to leave his place of work and stand in silence for one minute.'

Timmin made a rapid note on her hand terminal. 'I'll network that immediately.'

Morgus made a rapid calculation of how much a minute's loss of production across the board could cost the Conglomerate and said hurriedly. 'No, on second thoughts, better make that half a minute.'

Krau Timmin amended her note. 'Half a minute, sir.'

Proper sentiment was all very well, thought Morgus, as he returned to work, but business was business. The affair had been concluded with satisfactory despatch however; he made a mental note to reward the saboteur he had sent to Northcawl with a handsome bonus.

'He's mad, Doctor,' said Peri despairingly. 'Utterly mad!'

The Doctor nodded. 'And a raving egotist as well. He said my mind was nearly the equal of his. What incredible conceit!'

'Why do you think he hates this Morgus so much?'

'From the little I've seen of Morgus, I imagine Sharaz Jek's just one among many – ' The Doctor broke off as Salateen, the real Salateen, came into the workshop carrying two steaming plastic bowls on a tray. 'Ah, Salateen, I'd have known you anywhere! I'm the Doctor and this is Peri – '

'I know who you are,' interrupted Salateen.

'Yes, well,' said the Doctor cheerfully. 'I've been looking forward to this meeting.'

'Why?'

'Well, fellow prisoners and all that. How long have you been here?'

'Months,' said Salateen briefly. He carried the tray over to a workbench and slammed it down.

The Doctor and Peri came over to investigate. The bowls were filled with thick green slime, rather like decaying porridge.

Peri sniffed it dubiously. 'What is this stuff?'

'Nutrition.'

'Does it taste as bad as it looks?'

'Worse!'

Peri shuddered and pushed the bowl aside.

'Now then,' said the Doctor encouragingly. 'You probably know the best way out of here, eh?'

Salateen shook his head.

'Does that mean you don't know? Or you do and you won't tell us? We've got to escape.'

'It's impossible.'

The Doctor sighed, looking at Peri. 'Do you detect a certain coolness in our friend here?'

'Ice cold,' agreed Peri. 'I don't think he likes us.'

'*Like* you?' howled Salateen. 'Now that Sharaz Jek has you for company, he'll kill me.'

The Doctor raised his eyebrows. 'Kill you – surely you're – aah!'

Suddenly the Doctor rolled sideways onto his bench, arching his back in agony.

Peri ran to him. 'Doctor, what's wrong?'

'Cramp,' gasped the Doctor. 'Same as you had just now. Ouch!'

Peri massaged the Doctor's knotted shoulder muscles. 'There, is that better?'

Slowly the Doctor managed to straighten up.

Salateen was staring curiously at him. 'Do you mean to say you've *both* had cramp? You haven't touched a spectrox nest, have you?'

The Doctor and Peri looked at each other, both remembering Peri's fall when they had first entered the caves.

'A spectrox nest?' said the Doctor slowly. 'If by that you mean a kind of large, fuzzy, sticky ball . . .'

'You have!' Salateen threw back his head and laughed.

'What's so funny?' asked Peri indignantly.

'You're dying,' said Salateen simply. He laughed again.

The Doctor got up. 'What a marvellous sense of humour!' He grabbed Salateen by the shoulders and shook him till his teeth rattled. 'Try not to get hysterical. What do you mean, we're dying?'

Pulling away, Salateen made an effort to control himself. 'And Sharaz Jek thought he had company for life!' The thought almost set him off again, but a grim look from the Doctor encouraged him to calm down.

'Well?' demanded the Doctor.

In a shaking voice Salateen said, 'First there's a rash . . . Cramp is the second stage, then spasms, and finally a slow paralysis of the thoracic spinal nerve, then TDP.'

'What's TDP?' asked Peri uneasily.

'Thermal Death Point. It's called spectrox tox-aemia. I've seen dozens die from it.'

'But I thought spectrox preserved life?'

'When it's processed and refined, and adminis-tered in minute doses, then it does. In its raw state, especially in any quantity, it's a deadly poison.'

'What's the cure?' asked the Doctor hopefully.

'Oh, there's no cure,' Salateen chuckled. 'Wait till Jek finds out!'

Peri looked incredulously at the Doctor. 'He's kidding, isn't he?' She looked at Salateen's face, and then at the Doctor. 'No, I guess not.'

Salateen became serious at last. A little ashamedly he said, 'I'm sorry. I don't suppose you can see the funny side of it.'

Restraining himself with some effort, the Doctor said, 'Look, what exactly is a spectrox nest?'

'Spectrox is prepared from deposits left by the bat colonies, Doctor. The raw substance contains a chemical similar to mustard nitrogen, deadly to humans. That's why they use androids to collect the stuff and take it to the refinery for processing.'

'We haven't seen any bats.'

'They spend a chrysalid stage in the nest,' ex-plained Salateen. 'Three-year life cycle.'

The Doctor was thinking hard. 'There has to be some kind of antidote to this spectrox toxaemia. I mean, it sounds like a snake venom effect. There must be a serum or an antitoxin.'

'As a matter of fact there is,' said Salateen calmly.

'It was discovered by Professor Jackij, some years ago.'

'Well, don't keep us in suspense.'

'The snag is, Doctor, you need the milk from a queen bat. Trouble is, they go down into the deeps to hibernate, so you can't reach them.'

'Why not?' asked Peri.

'Well, for a start there's no oxygen down there, or almost none.'

'What else?' demanded the Doctor urgently. 'You said, "for a start".'

'There's some kind of creature . . . Probably lives in the magma and comes to the surface to hunt. It's a carnivore.'

'What's this creature like?' asked Peri.

Salateen shrugged. 'Nobody's ever run into one and lived to talk about it. All they ever find are its table leavings . . .'

Sharaz Jek was in his signal room, a small sub-cave packed with communications equipment, watching a light flash on a console. He touched a control. 'Yes?'

Stotz's voice came from a speaker. 'Jek? Stotz. I want a meet.'

'Why? You lost the cargo.'

'Your androids fouled up, Jek, not us.'

'I don't pay for undelivered goods.'

'Now listen, Jek,' snarled Stotz. 'If you don't pay for this consignment, we don't come back again – *ever*. Understand?'

'I can't keep this channel open. I'll meet you at shaft twenty-six in one hour.'

Even after Salateen's shattering news, the Doctor was still looking for a way out. 'This delightful process you describe, Major Salateen – how long does it take?'

'You're in the second stage now. You'll be dead in another two days.'

The Doctor considered the implications of this terrifying news. 'Then we can't afford to waste any more time here. We must get away.'

'Go through that door, Doctor,' said Salateen impressively, 'and you'll be dead in two seconds, not two days. There's an android permanently on guard out there. Sharaz Jek's androids are programmed to kill humans on sight.'

'We were brought here by two of Sharaz Jek's androids,' objected Peri.

'Oh, they can follow orders. But unless Jek commands otherwise, all humans without a belt-plate rank as targets. He even wears one himself.'

The Doctor rubbed his chin. 'How do these belt-plates work?'

'No idea.'

'They probably emit low frequency magma waves,' said the Doctor thoughtfully. 'Or even a neutrino pattern keyed to the android spectrum length.'

Sharaz Jek appeared through another door at the far end of the workshop. 'Congratulations,

Doctor. You understand something of android engineering?'

'Something,' said the Doctor modestly.

'In that case you will appreciate what a masterpiece is my facsimile of Salateen here.'

'Nearly perfect,' agreed the Doctor.

'Entirely perfect,' snarled Sharaz Jek.

Sharaz Jek's android masterpiece marched into General Chellak's office and saluted.

Chellak looked up. 'Yes, Major Salateen?'

'The engineers report increasing activity in the magma level, sir.'

The magma was the ever-boiling, seething semi-liquid core of the planet – what the Doctor had referred to as primeval mud.

'But surely the perihelion is weeks away?'

'The engineers say mud bursts can occur either side of the perihelion, General. It's a matter of internal pressures as well as gravity.'

'Do they actually think a burst is on the way?'

'They can't say yet, sir. It's just an early warning.'

General Chellak looked perplexed. It was bad enough having to cope with Sharaz Jek and his android rebels. Now he had to fight this unstable little world as well. 'What a planet! Very well. Set a party to work checking the mud barriers.'

These were the remote-controlled barriers capable of blocking selected tunnels. Their purpose was to channel the mud burst and provide an escape route for those unfortunate enough to be in the cave system when a mud burst erupted.

Salateen said, 'I took the liberty of ordering that to be done, sir. They're checking the barriers now.'

He saluted again and withdrew.

Chellak smiled wryly. Sometimes he thought that Salateen was too perfect – almost inhuman . . .

When Sharaz Jek re-entered the workshop he was wearing a cross-belt packed with ammunition pouches, and carrying a machine-pistol.

The Doctor surveyed him. 'Off to battle? What happens now?'

'I have to negotiate with my arms suppliers. They want full payment in spectrox for a shipment which I did not receive – or no more arms. I shall offer them half.'

'Well, if you have to go to arbitration,' said the Doctor helpfully, 'I have some experience – '

Sharaz Jek interrupted him. 'Your sense of humour will be the death of you, Doctor, probably quite soon.'

He moved away.

The Doctor shrugged. 'Emotional sort of fellow.'

'Why does he always wear that mask?' asked Peri.

Still in the doorway of the workshop, Sharaz Jek overheard her words and whirled round. He stalked towards Peri, seizing her by the arm. 'You want to know why? With your fair skin and beautiful features, you want to see the face under here – *do you*?'

58

Terrified, Peri shook her head.

Sharaz Jek released her. 'You are wise,' he whispered hoarsely. 'Even I cannot bear to see or touch myself. I who was once considered comely, who was always a lover of beauty.' His voice faltered, shaking with anguish. 'Now I have to live here in exile, live amongst androids, because androids do not see as we see.'

'What happened?' asked the Doctor quietly.

Sharaz Jek sent equipment crashing from a workbench with a sweeping gesture of rage and despair. 'Morgus!' he snarled. 'Why I ever trusted that Fescennine bag of slime.' His voice became calmer. 'We were partners, you see. Together we controlled the entire spectrox industry. Morgus's conglomerate owned the planet, and provided the financial backing. I designed and built an android work-force to collect and refine the spectrox. We had an agreement to share the profits equally – but once the operation was running smoothly, Morgus wanted everything for himself. He had already planned my death . . . The mud burst caught me without warning. How he must have gloated. But I tricked him – I reached one of the baking chambers and I *survived*.'

'You were – burned?' whispered Peri.

'Scalded near to death,' hissed Sharaz Jek. 'The flesh boiled, and hanging from the bones. But I lived – lived so that one day I could revenge myself upon that inhuman monster. *And so I shall!*' Abruptly Sharaz Jek turned and stalked away.

There was a moment of silence.

'Temperamental!' said the Doctor. 'More of a tennis player than a cricketer.'

'He didn't say why he blames Morgus,' said Peri. 'Just because he was caught in a mud burst . . .'

Any sympathy Salateen might have felt for Sharaz Jek had long since disappeared. 'I've heard that story a hundred times. Morgus supplied him with faulty detection instruments, so the mud burst caught Sharaz Jek by surprise. He didn't have time to get the mud-barriers down.'

'I see,' said the Doctor. He yawned and stretched. 'Well, I think it's time to be toddling along. Coming, Peri?'

'How can we leave – with an android guard outside?'

'Let's take a look,' suggested the Doctor calmly.

He headed for the door, and opened it, just far enough to peep through.

The door led to what looked like an armoury, a small chamber with its walls lined with weapon racks. At the other end of the little room, guarding the door, stood an android, covering the doorway to the workshop with a machine-pistol.

Peri joined the Doctor at the door. 'Satisfied?'

'The androids are programmed to kill humans, Peri. My physiology is quite different. The question is, will the android realise that?'

He went to the door.

Peri put a hand on his arm. 'Don't try it, Doctor.'

'Sorry, Peri, there's no alternative.'

The Doctor opened the door and stepped through into the armoury.

Salateen came to Peri's side. 'What does he mean? He isn't human?'

'Sssh!'

In the armoury the Doctor stood looking at the android. The single eye in the android's gleaming white head surveyed him in turn.

The Doctor took a step forward. The android levelled its weapon . . . and hesitated. The android was puzzled.

The creature before it presented the outward features of a human being, but some of the incoming data did not scan. The body temperature was wrong, and the internal construction was different. Humans did not have two hearts. But this creature did . . .

It looked human – but was it? Destroy – or ignore? The android lowered its weapon, confused.

The Doctor gave a sigh of relief. 'What a clever little android you are!' He slipped round behind it. 'Now we'll just cut out your solenoids. Don't worry, it won't hurt a bit.' He reached up and operated the cut-out switch in the back of the android's neck. It froze, motionless. 'All right, you two, you can come out now!'

Peri hurried into the armoury. 'Doctor, for a minute there I thought . . .' She shuddered.

The Doctor patted her shoulder. 'Me too! Never mind, it's all over now.' He took something from a shelf on the wall. 'What have we here?' It was a gold disc, bordered in red.

Salateen said eagerly, 'It's a spare belt-plate!'

The Doctor handed it to Peri. 'It might come in useful if we run into any more androids!' He headed for the exit.

'Where are you going?' called Salateen.

'To find those queen bats. We need their milk to cure us, remember?'

'I told you, Doctor, they're in the lower caves. There's no air down there.'

Peri looked worried, and the Doctor said, 'We'll collect some oxygenators from the TARDIS first. Come on.'

The Doctor and Peri moved away.

Snatching a machine-pistol from a wall rack, Salateen followed them.

6

The Magma Beast

Sharaz Jek and his android guards were already waiting by the time Stotz and his weary gun-runners trudged up to shaft twenty-six.

For a moment Stotz failed to see them. He started when the weirdly-masked figure appeared from the shadows. 'Jek!'

'Ah, there you are. I'm glad you were able to keep the rendezvous.'

Stotz moved closer to him. 'Damn you, Jek, this is the second time you've kept us waiting here three days. Then you only give me an hour's warning for a meet – '

'I am a busy man,' whispered Sharaz Jek. In fact, he made it a point of principle never to collect arms from the gun-runners until his Salateen android had confirmed that the chosen part of the cave system was completely clear of the constant Army patrols. If this policy resulted in the capture of the gun-runners, that would be most regretable. Sharaz Jek had no intention of putting himself at risk.

Stotz looked at Sharaz Jek's two androids, who

were carrying nothing except their machine-pistols. 'Okay, where's the spectrox?'

'In my store-room.'

'Now you listen to me, Jek. Five kilos is the price we fixed and five kilos is what I'm taking back to Androzani Major.'

'Why should I pay for weapons I never received? Why should I pay because you blundering idiots let the Army take them?'

'You'll pay, Jek, because we took the risk to get here on time. You'll pay because if you don't, we won't be doing business any more. Not so much as a single bullet. You'd be finished in a month without us. Wiped out. So you pay the full five kilos – or else!'

Sharaz Jek had been listening impassively to this tirade. 'Two kilos, Stotz.'

'Five.'

'It seems we are unable to reach an agreement. You'll have to try elsewhere for your spectrox.'

This remark underlined the weakness of Stotz's position. Sharaz Jek was the only source of spectrox, and Stotz knew it.

'Ah, come on, be reasonable, Jek.'

'Two kilos is very reasonable.'

'Everyone knows you cleared out the refinery stock-pile. You must be sitting on tons of the stuff.'

Stotz's eyes glistened at the thought of the unimaginable wealth in Sharaz Jek's hoard.

'And I know what it fetches, Stotz – per ounce. That's why your threats carry no weight. I can obtain weapons elsewhere.'

Stotz conceded defeat. 'The Boss isn't going to like this, Jek.'

'That is your problem.'

'Okay. Where's the two kilos?'

'I shall bring it to you in twenty minutes. Wait here.'

Sharaz Jek melted into the shadows, and his androids followed him.

'You really screwed him down there, eh, Stotzy?' sneered Krelper. 'Two kilos – what a deal!'

Stotz swung round angrily. 'Don't you try and get smart with me again, Krelper.' Krelper backed away, and Stotz went on thoughtfully, 'One thing we do know – now. That spectrox is stored somewhere, *within ten minutes from here.*'

'Yeah?'

'Yeah, Krelper. Tons and tons of spectrox, just waiting for guys like us to help ourselves.'

'We'd have to blow away Jek and his dummies first.'

Stotz tapped the belt-plate at his waist. 'We've got these, haven't we? The androids won't fire on us, not at first. I think Jek has fouled up in a big way this time. Come on!'

The Doctor and Peri were picking their way along a narrow gallery littered with scattered rocks, Salateen close behind them.

Peri had a nasty suspicion that they were lost. 'Where are we going, Doctor?'

'First we have to find our way back to the

TARDIS, and get the oxygenators. Then we go down to the lower levels and look for a hibernating queen bat – '

Suddenly a tall figure with a gleaming white head appeared from behind one of the rocks, machine-pistol in hand. It spotted Salateen, and fired immediately. Bullets blasted a chunk out of the rock just above the Doctor's head.

'Look out, Doctor,' screamed Peri.

Hit by the flying rock, the Doctor stumbled and fell, blood on his forehead.

Peri tried to run, but Salateen grabbed her from behind, swinging her in front of him as a shield.

The action wasn't as unchivalrous as it seemed. Recognising Peri's protective belt-plate the android lowered its weapon.

Pushing Peri in front of him, Salateen moved closer. Still holding Peri with one hand, Salateen raised his machine-pistol and fired past her, pumping bullet after bullet into the motionless android, which staggered but did not fall.

Suddenly the android's head exploded in flames. A lurid glow lit up the gallery as the android stood there still upright, blazing like a sort of two-legged torch.

Salateen dragged Peri past the android and on down the gallery, away from the unconscious Doctor.

'Let me go!' screamed Peri, but Salateen only tightened his grip, dragging her off into the darkness.

By the time the Doctor recovered and staggered to his feet they were out of sight. He looked at the android, still standing there. The fires of its blazing head were beginning to die down. 'Peri?' he called. 'Peri where are you?' He raised his voice. 'Salateen? Peri? Peri?'

There was no reply.

On the way to his strongroom, Sharaz Jek passed through his workshop – and saw with astonished rage that his captives were no longer there.

The absence of the Doctor and Salateen concerned him not at all – it was the loss of Peri that drove him into a frenzy. 'She has been taken from me,' he shrieked.

Smashing his fist upon a workbench, Sharaz Jek collapsed sobbing, masked head in his arms.

Still searching the caves for Peri, the Doctor passed through into a long narrow cave partly blocked with scattered boulders. He heard voices and the sounds of movement coming towards him. He ducked behind a rock, and peered out cautiously.

The far end of the cave rose upwards in a series of giant steps, and down these same steps came a small party of men. They wore an assortment of combat dress, some of them wore black berets, and they all carried machine-pistols . . .

Not soldiers, thought the Doctor, and not androids either. Which meant they must be the gunrunners.

He stayed where he was, in hiding, watching them.

Krelper was worried, and as usual he was whining about it.

Stotz's plan to follow Sharaz Jek and capture his entire stock of spectrox had seemed an attractive one at first. Now, moving through the gloomy caves towards unknown dangers, Krelper wasn't nearly so sure. 'We've lost him, Stotzy.'

Stotz looked round. 'He went this way I tell you.'

'He wouldn't have come down this deep.'

Ignoring him, Stotz moved on.

Strung out in single file, the gun-runners moved through the gallery. Suddenly a huge section of the rock wall seemed to detach itself, bearing down on the last man. He gave a terrified scream.

The attack had taken place opposite the Doctor's hiding place, and he could see the monster quite clearly. The body resembled that of a giant tortoise, or perhaps an armadillo, though the creature stalked upright on two powerful back legs, like a Tyrannosaurus Rex. The massive fanged head was like that of a tyrannosaurus too, though it also bore two ferocious-looking horns. The powerful arms were short and stubby, ending in two enormous claws.

As the monster stalked fowards, the massive carapace, at once protection and camouflage, covered the back of its body like an armoured cloak.

Crouched down, the Doctor guessed, the creature would easily pass for just another rounded boulder. Now it was upright and on the move, and it was hunting.

These thoughts flashed through the Doctor's mind in seconds.

Already the monster was attacking the unfortunate gun-runner, crushing him with its bulk and rending him with fangs and claws.

Hearing their fellow gun-runner's screams, Stotz and the others turned round, opening fire upon the monster.

The cave was filled with the harsh shattering roar of their machine-pistols, and the muzzle-flashes flared vividly in the gloom. A hail of bullets rained down on the monster's armoured carapace. Angered but apparently unhurt it abandoned its victim and swung round on these new attackers. It lumbered towards them, snarling, jaws slavering and clawed hands outstretched.

Unfortunately for the Doctor, the monster's course took it close to his hiding-place. Sensing fresh prey closer to hand, the monster swung round on the Doctor, roaring furiously.

7

Spy!

Luckily for the Doctor, the nearest of the gun-runners saw the monster's turning aside as a retreat. Emboldened, he leaped forward, blazing away with his machine-pistol at close range. The movement attracted the monster's attention. It swung round roaring, hurling itself upon its latest attacker.

The man went down screaming. The Doctor, quite unable to help him, dashed out from his hiding place and ran down the gallery, leaving the noise of battle behind him.

As the monster devoured its latest victim, Stotz and his two surviving gun-runners retreated the other way.

General Chellak looked up in astonishment as his office door was flung open and Salateen entered, dragging Peri behind him. Chellak noticed with some astonishment that his usually immaculate aide was grimy and dishevelled. He was brandishing a machine-pistol that was clearly not service

70

issue, and actually seemed to be in a state of some excitement.

'What the devil is going on, Salateen?'

'I'll explain in a minute, General.' Salateen closed and sealed the door, and shoved the exhausted Peri into a chair. 'One escaped prisoner, sir.'

'The android?'

Salateen nodded towards the rash that was spreading across Peri's legs. 'She's real enough. Androids' legs don't blister.' Salateen paused for a second, gathering his thoughts. He had a complicated and incredible story to tell, and very little time in which to convince Chellak of the truth. 'Sharaz Jek smuggled in copies of this girl and her friend, the Doctor.' He hesitated. 'And I'm afraid, sir, he also copied me.'

'Copied *you*?'

'I've been held prisoner in his camp for months, sir, ever since I was captured. What you thought was me was in fact an android. A spy for Sharaz Jek.'

Chellak gaped at him, unable to take in the incredible truth. 'You mean to say I've had an android for my aide all this time, without knowing it?'

'It's the truth, sir. When he made that copy of me it was like looking in a mirror. He's incredibly clever.'

'What a fool I've been!'

Peri slumped forwards, almost falling from her chair. Glancing at Chellak for permission, Salateen poured her a glass of water from the desk carafe.

'Don't blame yourself too much. That android has a cortex with over five million responses programmed into it. Jek boasted that it was his finest creation.'

Chellak was beginning to take in the full implication of Salateen's story. 'So Sharaz Jek has known every move, every plan we've made for months now, thanks to his android?'

'Within seconds, sir. The android is linked to his main computer.'

'Well, we'll soon put a stop to that!' Chellak flicked a switch on his desk-com. 'Major Salateen?'

Salateen reached forwards and closed the switch. 'Wait, sir. There's a better way. I thought of it on the way over . . .'

Suddenly, Salateen had the eerie experience of hearing his own voice coming from the speaker. 'Salateen here, sir. You called me?'

Chellak said, 'It's all right Major, I've found what I was looking for.'

'Very good, sir.'

Chellak sat back and looked at the real Salateen. 'You said there was a better way?'

'Disinformation, sir,' said Salateen simply.

'Using the android?'

'As long as Jek doesn't discover I've made it back here, he'll believe everything the android relays into the terminal!'

Chellak smiled, stroking his moustache. 'You're a wily fellow, Salateen, I've always said so. What exactly do you suggest?'

'We can make him think we're moving in one direction when in fact we're moving in on his base. I know the way.'

'I like that idea, Major Salateen. I like it very much. Meanwhile, of course, you and the girl will have to stay out of sight. You can use my private quarters . . .'

Once they were convinced they were far enough from the monster to be safe, Stotz and his gun-runners slowed down their pace. Suddenly they found Sharaz Jek and two androids barring their path, at a point where a wooden stairway led up to the higher levels, and down to the lower.

The sinister masked figure surveyed the bedraggled gun-runners with ironic amusement. 'So, you thought to follow me? I expected that. Now you have learned the price of your curiosity.'

Stotz glared at him, his chest still heaving from the frantic dash through the caves. 'Is that thing back there one of your pets?'

'The magma beasts never ascend above Blue Level. In any case, they have no taste for my androids. Only flesh and blood.'

'You tricked us,' accused Krelper hoarsely. 'You led us into that!'

'You were led by your own cupidity. Greed, heedless of caution, lures many a man to his death.'

The sensors of one of Sharaz Jek's androids detected movement on the level just above them. It swung round, aiming its machine-pistol.

73

'Whoever you are, come out!' called Jek.

Slowly the Doctor appeared at the top of the stairway. Resignedly, he raised his hands.

Beneath his mask, Sharaz Jek's lips twisted into a smile. 'Doctor! I had not expected to see you again so soon.'

'Life often springs these little surprises,' said the Doctor. He came down the steps.

'Bring him,' said Sharaz Jek, and led the way down into the darkness.

After a short but complicated journey through the lower levels, the Doctor found himself back in Sharaz Jek's workshop, guarded by both androids and gun-runners.

Sharaz Jek looked curiously at him. 'Tell me Doctor, how is it that you were able to walk past my androids?'

The Doctor had no intention of telling the truth – the ability might well come in useful once again. 'I don't know, maybe they just liked my face.'

An android entered, a plastic bag of white crystals in each hand. Sharaz Jek turned to Stotz. 'Take your spectrox. Two kilos, as agreed.'

Stotz nodded to Krelper, who moved forwards nervously, taking the bags from the android and hurriedly stepping back.

Stotz glared angrily at Sharaz Jek. 'The suppliers aren't going to like this, Jek.'

'Then tell them that if they will supply gas

weapons as agreed, and deliver them safely, I will pay eight kilos for the next shipment.'

Suddenly Sharaz Jek's arm swept out, and he smashed his open hand to the side of the Doctor's neck. The Doctor staggered and almost fell, but he recovered himself, and looked back at Jek unafraid.

'When I ask a question, Doctor, I do not expect flippancy,' whispered Sharaz Jek. 'Where is the girl? Where is Peri?'

The Doctor rubbed his aching neck. 'I wish I knew.'

Sharaz Jek nodded to the androids. 'Take him.'

Two androids closed in on the Doctor.

'Tear his arms out – slowly,' ordered Jek.

Each android took one of the Doctor's arms, and soon he was stretched out between them, like the rope in a tug-of-war. 'You know the power an android can exert, Doctor,' said Sharaz Jek softly. 'After your arms, they will remove your legs. Now, where is the girl?'

The Doctor felt his shoulder joints beginning to crack. 'I don't know,' he gasped. 'We got into a shoot-out with one of your androids.'

Suddenly Sharaz Jek seemed to lose control. 'You can't protect her,' he shrieked. 'I shall tear the truth out of you!'

'I think she's with Salateen,' gasped the Doctor. 'That's all I know . . .'

This time Sharaz Jek believed him. 'Release him!' The androids released the Doctor's arms and he collapsed in a heap, rubbing his aching shoulder joints.

'Salateen!' whispered Sharaz Jek. 'In that case, they've probably reached the Army HQ.'

The Doctor looked up at him. 'If they have, then it's round two to the Army, I'd say.'

'You know nothing,' sneered Sharaz Jek. He began pacing about the workshop, muttering obsessively. 'I must find her. I must get the girl back . . .'

Stotz indicated the Doctor. 'What about him?'

'He is of no interest to me now.'

'Then I think I'd like to take him back to Major with us. The Boss will want to question him. I think he's a spy – why else would he be snooping around?'

Stotz didn't really care if the Doctor was a spy or not. He was anxious to salvage what little credit he could from this disastrous trip, and the capture of a spy would at least be something in his favour.

Sharaz Jek glanced indifferently down at the Doctor. 'He told me he was – ' He broke off. 'It is of no matter what he is. If you want him, take him. I must find the girl.'

Followed by his androids, Sharaz Jek hurried from the workshop.

Stotz heaved the Doctor to his feet. 'When we get back to Major, you're going to wish those androids had finished the job,' he said gloatingly. 'You'll be worked over by experts there.'

The Doctor was dragged away.

* * *

76

Although there is only one cure for spectrox toxaemia, it is possible to counteract the effects, at least for a while.

Salateen was in the process of shooting a powerful stimulant into the unconscious Peri's bloodstream.

They were in General Chellak's private quarters; the tiny bedroom and bathroom adjoining the General's office was one of the privileges of rank.

The injection-gun gave a faint pop, and there was a brief glow on Peri's wound. She came suddenly back to consciousness. She looked around her, struggling to take in her surroundings. 'What's happening?' she muttered. 'Where am I?'

Salateen clapped his hand over her mouth. 'Sssh!' He looked anxiously at the thin wall dividing them from the office.

In the office Chellak was concluding a briefing session with his aide – the android Major Salateen. The information content of the briefing had been carefully chosen to deceive Sharaz Jek.

'No further orders, Major,' concluded General Chellak.

But the android's keen ears had caught the suppressed muttering from the adjoining room. It turned slowly, staring at the wall. Its x-ray vision penetrated the thin partition, showing Peri stretched out on the bunk, with Salateen beside her, his hand still over her mouth.

'I said no further orders,' repeated Chellak.

'Very good, sir,' said the android Salateen. It stared at the wall for a moment longer, then turned, looking impassively at the General.

Now that he knew the truth, Chellak wondered how he could ever have been deceived. To cover his nervousness he snapped, 'Well, was there anything else?'

'The magma pressure is still increasing,' said the android levelly.

Chellak shrugged. 'It's been high before without anything happening. I'm sure the engineers will give us ample warning if there's a mud burst on the way.'

'There should be time to get the barriers down sir. But a sudden burst could wipe out our forward patrols.'

'That's a calculated risk, Major. We cannot suspend all forward operations because sometime during the next month there might be a mud burst.'

The android's mouth twitched in the half-smile that was so typical of Salateen. 'No, sir, of course not.'

Chellak sat marvelling at Sharaz Jek's skill.

The android saluted and left the office.

Chellak turned and hurried into his quarters. 'That android suspects something.'

Salateen nodded uneasily. 'They can detect human body heat even through a wall,' he said – unaware that the android's x-ray vision had already uncovered their secret.

Chellak said, 'We'll have to get it off the base

somehow, that's the only thing for it!' He glanced down at Peri. 'How do you feel?'

Peri felt sick and dizzy and her body was racked with shooting pains. 'Awful. Not that you care.'

Chellak tilted her head back, raising an eyelid with his thumb. He studied the eyeball for a moment, then turned away. 'I don't think she'll be any use to us.'

'I'll give her another injection in an hour, sir,' said Salateen. 'She'll make it.'

They might have been talking about a sick horse, thought Peri, or a broken-down car. 'You two are all heart,' she muttered.

Chellak glared down at her. 'If you weren't dying anyway, I'd probably have you shot. You may not have been gun-running, but any dealings with the enemy are punishable by death.'

'Dealings with the enemy? What dealings?'

'Sharaz Jek went to great lengths to rescue you and your friend the Doctor from execution. He didn't do that out of kindness.'

'Look,' said Peri desperately. 'The Doctor and I were just as much Sharaz Jek's prisoners as Salateen here. And if it hadn't been for the Doctor we'd all still be his prisoners now.'

'That is actually true sir,' confirmed Salateen.

Defeated in logic, Chellak took refuge in authority. 'Well, it's academic now anyway. I just want her fit enough to guide one of the first assault-groups.'

'Fat chance the way I feel,' muttered Peri.

But no one was listening to her.

The Doctor's captors led him steadily upwards, until they reached a long ravine that rose steeply to the surface.

The Doctor raised his head, drinking in the fresh, dry air. Shafts of desert sunlight pierced down through the gloom.

A dull roaring came from just beyond the end of the ravine. 'What's that?' asked the Doctor feebly.

'Our ship,' said Stotz with satisfaction. 'Right on time. Hurry it up.'

The Doctor sank slowly to the ground. 'Can't,' he gasped. 'My legs seem to be going numb. I suppose that's stage three.'

'Stage three of what?'

'I believe it's called spectrox toxaemia.'

Stotz stared at him. 'You've been messing around with raw spectrox?'

'Yes,' said the Doctor painfully. 'Why don't you just leave me here to die?'

For a moment Stotz seemed to consider it, but then he shook his head. 'You'll last long enough for questioning.' He heaved the Doctor brutally to his feet. 'Take his other arm, Krelper, we'll be at the ship in a few minutes.'

Krelper grabbed the Doctor's arm. 'Come on, you. Move!'

The Doctor was dragged towards his uncertain fate.

8

The Boss

Chellak was examining the belt-plate which Sala-teen had taken from Peri. It was a gold disc with a red border, studded around the edge.

'How does it work?'

'Apparently it emits a low-frequency signal,' said Salateen. 'Something the androids recognise as friendly.'

Chellak returned the disc. 'Seems simple enough. If our artificers could knock up a few hundred of these . . .'

'That's what I thought, sir.'

'Right,' said Chellak decisively. 'We'll attend to it as soon as I've got that android off the base.'

'How will you do that, sir?'

'Send it on a fool's errand, well out of the way.'

Salateen said, 'Anything you tell the android will be known to Jek within seconds. It will have to sound convincing or he'll get suspicious.'

Chellak gave him an irritated look. 'Yes, Major, I realise that. What do you suggest?'

Salateen said thoughtfully. 'Perhaps you could

reinforce what you say by putting a call through to Trau Morgus? If you tell Morgus you've located Jek's headquarters and give out a set of bogus co-ordinates – '

'We can circle round and catch the beggar napping,' completed Chellak enthusiastically. 'That's very good, Salateen.'

'Jek will automatically believe anything he hears you discussing with Morgus, sir. He's got a tap on the interplanetary vid. He can pick up all transmissions between here and Androzani Major.'

'How long has he been intercepting our transmissions?'

'I think the android put the tap in, sir.'

Chellak shook his head wearily. 'It's no wonder this campaign has been getting nowhere. Sharaz Jek has had advance warning of every operation we've planned!'

'Yes, sir. But we've got him cold this time.'

'Yes, I think we have, Major Salateen,' said Chellak with evident satisfaction. 'And before he's executed, I'll see that evil renegade dragged in chains through every city on Androzani Major'

The gun-runners' space-ship had landed in a hidden valley. It was a stubby cylindrical affair; three projecting fins on either side showed that it was designed for atmospheric flight. Little more than a shuttle-craft, thought the Doctor, designed to run to and fro between the twin planets.

He was hustled up the ramp and handcuffed to a

metal ventilation grille in the tiny cluttered control room, his hands behind him.

Stotz settled himself in the central pilot chair, while Krelper operated the co-pilot console.

'Height?' snapped Stotz.

'One twenty metres.'

'Lock on course.'

'Course set, lock on.'

'Okay . . . close jumps.'

'Close jumps.' Krelper stepped back from the console. 'That's it, Stotz. Androzani Major here we come!'

The little ship shuddered briefly and took off without fuss.

Stotz sank back in the pilot chair, and yawned and stretched. 'Right, you lads go and get some rest.'

'I reckon we deserve it!'

'Off you go then. I'll just tell the Boss, we're on our way.'

Krelper and the other gun-runner, a taciturn type called Stark, filed out of the room.

The Doctor had been watching this with some puzzlement, wondering why Stotz was being so solicitous of his men. His suspicions were confirmed when Stotz went to the door and locked it. 'Afraid of intruders?' called the Doctor.

Stotz unwrapped the headband he wore on his forehead. 'When I talk to the Boss, it's got to be just the two of us. That's the way he likes it.'

The Doctor winced as the grimy cloth was tied

across his eyes. 'Something wrong with his face – or mine?'

Ignoring the bound and blindfolded Doctor, Stotz crossed to his video transceiver and punched in a coded signal.

A light flickered on Morgus's desk – the one signal that could not be ignored. He touched the remote control that sealed the door, then switched on the vid.

The picture-window clouded and then the head and shoulders of Stotz appeared, so clearly that Morgus's office window seemed to be looking into ths gun-runners' space-ship.

'You're late, Stotz,' said Morgus flatly.

'We ran into some trouble, sir. The Army intercepted the consignment.'

'I know that. The weapons were untraceable.'

'I made doubly sure,' boasted Stotz. 'We counter-attacked, wiped out the Army patrol and destroyed the weapons. Then we had trouble with Sharaz Jek.'

'He refused to pay, I suppose?'

'Two kilos, instead of five.'

If Stotz hoped for praise, he was disappointed. 'It should have been four at least, Stotz.'

'Ah, but I forced him to agree more for the next delivery, sir. He's desperate for more gas weapons – so I said eight kilos, or no deal.'

'Eight? Did he agree?'

'Of course he did. He could see I meant business.

And another thing,' said Stotz, gaining confidence, 'I've got a fix on where the spectrox is stored.'

'Now that information could be very valuable – ' Morgus broke off as he took in the blindfolded figure behind Stotz. 'Who's that?'

'A Government snoop, sir. We caught him spying.'

'Take off the blindfold.'

Stotz obeyed and stepped aside.

Morgus stared at the vid-screen.

The Doctor blinked, recognizing the cold-faced little man. 'Ah, so it is you, Morgus. I thought I recognised the voice!'

'Something is happening I do not understand,' said Morgus. He was filled with a kind of nameless dread, a fear that somehow events were slipping out of his control.

'He calls himself the Doctor, sir,' said Stotz.

'I know that, Stotz. Be quiet. I need time to think.'

Morgus swung round, away from the screen, staring into space. He spoke quietly, almost inaudibly, trying to clarify his thoughts by speaking them out loud. 'The execution was a hoax. The General is obtuse, but he is a loyal servant of the Government. He would not have deceived me unless . . . unless his orders came from some higher authority.' Having reached this impeccably logical and totally incorrect conclusion, Morgus turned back to the screen. 'Who is your employer, Doctor? Who are you acting for?'

'I'm not acting for anyone,' said the Doctor

wearily. 'I was just passing through, and I got caught up with this pathetic little local war.'

Morgus leaned back in his chair. 'I am the richest man in the whole of the Five Planets, Doctor. Tell me the truth, and I will reward you beyond your wildest dreams.'

'I *am* telling the truth! I *keep* telling the truth. Why is it nobody believes me?'

'He's a Government snoop, I tell you, sir,' snarled Stotz. 'Stick a few electrodes into him, he'll soon talk.'

There was an edge of panic in Morgus's voice. 'If he'd been sent to Minor by the Government, I would know. My source on the Praesidium would have told me. No, somebody in a very high position must have ordered Chellak to fake the execution.'

'How do you know it was faked?' asked the Doctor unhelpfully. 'Maybe they were just bad shots.'

By now Morgus was building a second mistaken conclusion upon the first. 'The President! It can only have been the President. Something must have aroused his suspicion.' Suddenly Morgus felt events crowding in on him. He must have time to think, to plan . . . 'Stotz, I want you to lock your ship in geo-stationary orbit. I don't want you back here on Major until I've had time to consider all the implications of this affair.'

He reached out and snapped off the vid-screen.

Stotz jabbed savagely at his control panel. 'Geo-stationary orbit!' He glared round at the Doctor.

'And if it wasn't for you we'd be well on our way home. I should've wiped you the first minute I saw you.' He stamped out of the control room, and the door closed behind him.

The Doctor stood quite still for a moment, considering what he had learned. So, Morgus, a powerful figure behind the Government, and Sharaz Jek's deadly foe, was also the employer of the gun-runners thus supporting the rebellion. Somehow Morgus was playing each side against the other to his own advantage.

Time to worry about that later, decided the Doctor. The thing to do now was to escape.

He began heaving at the link-chain on the handcuffs that bound him to the metal grille.

Chellak was studying the belt-plate that had been taken from Peri, when he heard the Salateen android approaching. Hastily he swept the belt-plate into a drawer. He looked up as the android entered. 'Ah, Major Salateen. I have a treat for you. It's some time since you've been out on a field operation, isn't it?'

The android looked impassively at him. 'Yes, sir.'

'I know how bored an officer of your temperament must get stuck on HQ duties.' Chellak paused. 'Now as you know, we've had a satellite monitoring radio signals here for some time. We have now located a transmitter which must belong to the rebels – just here!'

Chellak rose, and pointed to the wall-map of the cave system. 'Make a note of the co-ordinates.'

The Salateen android studied the map. 'That's several miles away sir, and bad narrows all the way.'

The narrows, deep ravines that linked the various cave systems, were a constant hazard in field operations. They formed a series of natural bottle-necks, easy to watch and guard, and perfect places for an ambush by either side.

'Exactly,' said Chellak. 'Probably the reason Jek chose that position. Anyway, we've got to tackle it. I want you to take a small team, good men, and do a recce. As soon as I receive confirmation, I'll mount an attack in force.' He looked hard at the android, still scarcely able to believe that it wasn't human. 'All right?'

'Of course, sir,' said the android smoothly. 'I'll get the operation under way immediately.'

In the control room of Stotz's space-ship, in orbit around Androzani Major, the Doctor was still struggling desperately to free himself.

The handcuff-chain was linked around two of the thin bars that formed the grille, and for what seemed like a very long time, the Doctor had been bending the bars to and fro, trying to induce a fracture by means of metal fatigue.

Suddenly one of the bars snapped with an audible report. The Doctor froze, looking at the door. If Stotz heard the noise and came running to investigate . . . But he didn't.

No one came.

Much encouraged, the Doctor set to work on the second bar.

A small group of soldiers in full battle kit moved along through the caves, heading north. The android Salateen was in the lead.

Suddenly he stopped and stepped aside, waving the men on past him. 'Carry on, Sergeant, keep the men moving. I'll catch you up.'

As the men moved away, the android turned back to the shadowed cleft where its sensors had detected a lurking figure.

Sharaz Jek stepped out of the darkness. 'Chellak is sending you north. He is trying to deceive me as to his true intentions.'

'Yes, Master.'

'Have you seen the girl?'

'Chellak has hidden her in his private quarters, with Major Salateen.'

Sharaz Jek nodded. 'But now you are out of the camp, Salateen will feel free to move about ... Excellent! There is a chance that the girl will be alone.'

In his office, Chellak was carrying out the second part of Major Salateen's plan. He was about to send false information to Morgus in the hope that Sharaz Jek, tapping the interplanetary vid, would believe the false information to be true. He punched up the code for a call to Morgus.

* * *

On Androzani Major, Morgus was still trying to work out a plan that would leave him safe, unsuspected and victorious.

The com-unit on his desk buzzed discreetly. Morgus went back to his desk and touched the vid-control, accepting the call.

The window clouded, and Chellak's face appeared. 'Good news, Trau Morgus. Our radio satellite has pin-pointed Sharaz Jek's base.'

'You are certain?'

'Yes, Trau Morgus. I am mobilising to attack now. In approximately six hours we shall be in position for a full-scale assault.'

'If you know where Sharaz Jek's base is now, why waste six hours?'

'There are many difficult narrows to traverse. It will take that time to assemble our men and move them into position.'

'Have you informed the President?'

'Not yet. I believe his Excellency is at a meeting of the Praesidium.'

'Yes,' said Morgus rapidly. 'Yes, he is. I am seeing him myself, after the meeting. I will tell him the good news myself. Thank you for reporting, General, and well done!'

'Thank you, sir!'

The image of Chellak faded from the screen, and Morgus resumed his staring out of the window.

Like many tightly-controlled people, Morgus was all the more prone to panic once the control started to slip. Was Chellak telling him the whole truth? Or was it all part of some cunning plan to entrap him? By now, Morgus was rapidly convincing himself that desperate measures were necessary.

When the second bar on the grille finally snapped, it seemed to make even more noise than the first, but once again, no one seemed to hear. Perhaps the exhausted gun-runners were all fast asleep, thought the Doctor hopefully.

At last he was free, but it was a very limited freedom, his hands cuffed behind him.

First things first, thought the Doctor. He looked round for a way to get rid of the handcuffs. His eyes brightened as he caught sight of the ship's gyro-control stabiliser.

This particular model incorporated a short vertical laser-beam that ran between the twin poles of the stabiliser. The beam was protected by a transparent plasti-steel tube.

The Doctor regarded the instrument throughtfully. There must be some way of removing the tube for adjustment and repair.

Raising one leg he jabbed at the control panel with his foot. To the Doctor's delight the tube slowly retracted, leaving the bright-blue laser-beam exposed.

The Doctor shuffled round till he had his back to the beam, and then extended his chained wrists.

In his hurry he miscalculated slightly, and the laser-beam touched one of his wrists. He jerked away, stifling a yell at the searing pain.

Recovering himself, he drew a deep breath and repeated the operation, much more slowly and carefully this time.

The steel chain linking the Doctor's wrists came closer and closer to the fierce blue beam.

It touched, there was a fierce buzz and a shower of sparks, and the steel chain fell apart like a snapped cobweb. With infinite care, the Doctor used the laser-beam to cut the metal cuffs from his wrists.

At last he was free.

The question was now, what should he do with his freedom?

9

Crash-down

Peri lay half-dozing on the bunk in Chellak's private quarters. She opened her eyes. Gloomily she studied the strange mottling on her legs. It seemed to be spreading.

Two injections of Salateen's stimulant had undoubtedly had an effect, and for the time at least Peri was feeling much better, though the drug had left her faintly drowsy and dry-mouthed. But eventually her symptoms would be bound to return.

Peri began wondering how long it would be before the shooting pains and dizziness came back. She began wondering how much longer she had to live . . .

She sank back on the bunk and fell into a kind of half-sleep. She wasn't sure how long it lasted – but when she opened her eyes it was to a nightmare.

Sharaz Jek was bending over her.

Peri stared at him and opened her mouth to scream. As she drew breath, Sharaz Jek clamped a white pad soaked in some fluid over her mouth and nostrils. She struggled wildly for a moment and then went limp.

Sharaz Jek lifted her body tenderly in his arms and moved away.

Perhaps because of his weakened condition it took the Doctor quite some time to get the hang of the controls. He had been holding the effects of the spectrox toxaemia at bay by sheer will power, refusing to give in. Nevertheless, his body was periodically racked by spasms of cramp, and he had to struggle furiously against recurring waves of dizziness.

'Right,' muttered the Doctor at last. 'First thing is to get that door locked.'

This achieved, he turned his attention back to the actual controls. 'Now then . . . auto-hold off . . .' With a distressing lurch, the ship left its geostationary orbit.

'That's it. And now, a return course for Androzani Minor followed by a vertical descent pattern to the planet's surfacr . . .'

The ship lurched again and settled into its new course.

Wearily the Doctor leaned back in the high-backed pilot chair and awaited events.

Someone was bound to notice something, sooner or later.

'An attempt to assassinate *me*?' said the President horrified. 'Who told you of this, Morgus?'

'A man in my position has sources all over the world. It is of course only a whisper, but I think it would be wise to act with caution.'

'Yes indeed,' agreed the President fervently. 'You have no idea who the miscreants might be?'

'Not at the moment, Excellency, but I am hoping for more definite information soon.'

'I must strengthen my bodyguard,' muttered the President.

'I would take other precautions, sir,' whispered Morgus confidentially. 'Vary your routine. Cease to announce forthcoming engagements. In fact, for the time being, it might be well for you to cancel all your public appearances.'

'Yes,' said the President thoughtfully. 'Yes, that might seem prudent under the circumstances.'

Morgus rose. 'I'll have your floater brought round to the side entrance, Excellency,' he said conspiratorially. 'You may leave the building by my private lift.'

The President rose in turn. 'Thank you, Morgus. I cannot tell you how much I appreciate this.'

Morgus smiled. 'Your Excellency's safety is my sole concern.'

They were standing by the lift door now, and Morgus reached out and touched the control.

As the concealed door slid open, Morgus held out his right hand as if to clasp the President's hand in farewell.

The President was surprised. It was unlike Morgus to make such an emotional gesture.

He was even more surprised when Morgus con-
verted the gesture into a flat-handed shove on the
chest that sent him staggering through the lift
doorway.

There was no lift – just the empty shaft. Morgus
peered over the edge, and caught a glimpse of the
President's body spinning towards the ground a
hundred stories below. It took him a surprisingly
long time to reach the bottom.

Morgus turned away, and summoned Krau
Timmin. Minutes later she appeared in the doorway, cool, blonde and elegant as ever.

'Krau Timmin, the most appalling thing has
happened,' said Morgus solemnly. 'His Excellency
. . .' He gestured towards the lift door.

Timmin's eyes widened. 'Not the President?'

Morgus nodded. 'It was all over in a second. I
had no time to stop him. This is a tragic loss to the
world.'

'Dreadful, sir,' agreed Krau Timmin. 'And that it
should have happened in this building!'

'Yes, yes,' said Morgus impatiently. 'I am deeply
distressed, Krau Timmin.'

'Naturally sir, you must be.' The total lack of
emotion in her voice matched Morgus's own.

'Still, it could have been worse,' continued
Morgus.

'In what way, sir?'

'It might have been me. You had better tell the
members of the Praesidium the sad news.'

'Yes, sir.'

'In the absence of the President,' Morgus went on impressively, 'I myself am flying to Androzani Minor immediately on a peace mission.'

'A peace mission, sir?'

'Yes. As Chairman of the Sirius Conglomerate, I shall negotiate with Sharaz Jek to end this horrible carnage.'

'The world will be forever in your debt, Trau Morgus.'

Morgus smiled. The banal phrase had defined precisely the situation he was planning to achieve. 'Yes, yes, quite so. Have my private jet ready in ten minutes.'

'Yes, sir.'

She turned to leave. Morgus's voice halted her at the door. 'Oh, and Krau Timmin – have the lift engineer shot, will you?'

Emotionlessly, Krau Timmin made a note on her hand-terminal and left.

After all, thought Morgus, it was only just. The man had demanded a disgustingly high bribe for adjusting the circuits so the door in his office would open with the lift still at the bottom . . . An immediate execution would punish his greed – and ensure his silence.

An android strode into Sharaz Jek's workroom, the still unconscious Peri in its arms. Sharaz Jek followed close behind them.

At a nod from its master, the android laid Peri carefully down on an empty workbench.

Sharaz Jek waved it away. 'Good. Return to your position.'

Moving to his video surveillance console, Sharaz Jek made a few rapid adjustments to the controls. Somewhere in Chellak's HQ the lens on a hidden spy-camera slid smoothly forwards.

Sharaz Jek studied the picture on one of his screens. It showed a group of soldiers in full combat-gear being issued with oval discs which they clamped to their belts.

Sharaz Jek turned away.

He took a phial of liquid from a shelf and went back to Peri. Removing the stopper, he forced a few drops of the liquid between her open lips. Peri choked and spluttered and opened her eyes. Sharaz Jek handed her the phial. 'Drink this, you'll feel better.'

Propping herself up on one elbow, Peri sipped from the phial, which contained some kind of fiery cordial.

She looked round the familiar gloomy surroundings.

'Back again, I see,' she said weakly.

Sharaz Jek loomed over her, his voice unexpectedly gentle. 'I'm sorry it was necessary to drug you. The after-effects will soon pass.'

'Have you seen the Doctor?'

'The Doctor?' Sharaz Jek said dismissively. 'Oh yes, the Doctor's gone, to Androzani Major.'

'I don't believe it!'

'You'll soon forget him, Peri.'

Peri struggled to sit up. 'He wouldn't leave me here. He wouldn't!'

'He had no choice,' said Jek dryly. 'Some people I do business with decided to take him with them.'

'But why?'

'They believed he was spying on them for the Govenment.'

'But that's ridiculous!'

Sharaz Jek shrugged. 'These petty criminals are invariably paranoid, their twisted little minds infested with mistrust and suspicion.'

'You didn't have to let them take him,' sobbed Peri. 'You could have stopped them.'

Sharaz Jek didn't seem to hear her. 'To think that I, Sharaz Jek, who once mixed with the highest in the land, am now dependent upon the very dregs of society. Base, perverted scum, who contaminate everything they touch. And it is Morgus who brought me to this. Morgus destroyed my life.' He whirled round on Peri, eyes blazing through the slits of his mask. 'Do you think I'm mad?'

Peri shook her head. 'No . . .'

'I am mad,' said Jek, with quiet satisfaction. 'Do I frighten you?'

'No,' whispered Peri again, although by now she was terrified.

Sharaz Jek leaned over her, the hideously masked face close to her own. 'You are so important to me. I have lived so long in these caves, alone, like an animal. But now I can feast my eyes on your delicacy and forget the pain and the blackness in my mind. That is all in the past. Now we can think of the future.'

He reached out, gently stroking her hair.

Peri was dimly aware that this fantastic, twisted being was making some kind of declaration of love. She gazed around the gloomy workshop. If this was all that lay ahead of her, it was almost a relief to recall that she was dying.

'What future?' said Peri wearily. 'You know the Army are planning to attack you.'

'I know.'

'And your androids won't fire back because the soldiers will be wearing belt-plates.'

'Belt-plates emitting a signal on eighty beta-cycles. I have changed the recognition code to fifty beta-cycles.' There was a hideous glee in Sharaz Jek's voice. 'General Chellak, my dear, is in for a shock.

General Chellak was receiving a shock at this very moment. He had just discovered that Peri was missing from his quarters. He looked at Major Salateen in amazement. 'She's gone.'

'She must have been stronger than we thought, sir.'

Chellak shrugged. 'Well, she can't get far, can she? We'll soon pick her up again – unless she dies first of course.'

They went back into Chellak's office and began going over the plans for the attack.

* * *

Shaking his head to clear it, the Doctor looked at the forward view-screen built into the control console. Androzani Minor seemed to be rushing towards him at alarming speed. Too fast, thought the Doctor. Much too fast . . . He rubbed his eyes, trying to concentrate.

Suddenly there came a pounding at the door. 'Doctor. Unlock this door! What are you doing in there?' There was more pounding, then Stotz's voice came again. 'Doctor? Are you going to open this door or not?'

The Doctor was beginning to feel rather light-headed. 'Ah, Stotzy! Have a nice rest?'

'Damn you, Doctor, open this door!'

'Sorry, seems to be locked!'

The Doctor heard Stotz call, 'Krelper, go and get the cutting gear!' Then, 'Doctor? Now listen, Doctor, be reasonable. This isn't going to do you any good!'

The Doctor glanced at the screen, now entirely filled by the planetary surface. 'Sorry, we'll be touching down in about two minutes. Or more probably crashing down! You see I'm a bit out of practice with manual landings. So if I were you Stotzy, I'd find something firm to hang on to!'

'I'll murder you when I get in there, Doctor,' bellowed Stotz.

Seconds later, the Doctor heard a hissing sound from the control-room door. He glanced round and saw the glowing tip of a thermic lance carving through the metal of the cabin door like a red-hot knife-tip through rice-paper.

With astonishing speed the lance sliced a jagged square panel out of the door. Punched from the outside, the panel dropped into the control room with a clang.

Through the resultant gap the Doctor saw an enraged Stotz, glaring at him. Stotz reached his hand through the hole to open the door and gave a yell of agony as his wrist touched the still red-hot rim of the gap.

Abandoning the idea, he levelled his machine-pistol at the Doctor. 'All right, snoop. Hands in the air. Come over here and open that door.'

'Why?'

'Because I'll kill you if you don't!'

The Doctor laughed. 'Not a very persuasive argument, actually, Stotz, because I'm going to die anyway. Unless of course . . .'

'I'll give you till a count of three,' screamed Stotz. 'One!'

Quite unperturbed the Doctor went on. 'Unless of course I can find the antidote . . .'

'Two!'

'I owe it to my friend Peri to try because I got her into this. So you see, I'm not going to let you stop me now!'

The Doctor closed his eyes.

On the screen, the surface of Androzani Minor rushed closer . . .

10

Mud Burst!

'Three!' yelled Stotz.

His finger tightened on the trigger – and the ship slammed into the desert surface of Androzani Minor.

Stotz was thrown back, clear across the corridor.

The Doctor stabbed at the controls, opening the door on the far side of the room and the exit hatch beyond.

By the time Stotz got the door open and came running into the control room the Doctor was out of the ship and haring across the desert.

Krelper and Stark, the other surviving gunrunner, came tumbling into the control room behind Stotz.

'Get after him!' yelled Stotz, and waved them onwards.

Something jingled against Stotz's foot.

He picked it up. It was a section of broken twisted handcuff. Angrily Stotz hurled it across the control room.

* * *

The Doctor was sprinting like a hare across the bare and sandy desert surface of Androzani Minor, with Krelper and Stark at his heels.

Every now and again, the bullets from their machine-pistols kicked up spurts of sand close to the Doctor's body. However, since the Doctor was ducking and weaving and the gun-runners found it hard to run and shoot straight at the same time, none of the bullets hit him.

The Doctor ran into an area of dunes and was at last able to find some cover.

Krelper and Stark came to a halt, scanning the country ahead of them.

'That way,' shouted Krelper. 'He went down that ridge!'

The Doctor popped into sight behind a distant dune, and then disappeared again.

'Come on,' yelled Krelper. 'After him. Get him!'

Stumbling and clumsy in the soft sand, the two gun-runners ran after the Doctor.

An alarm-light flashed on Stotz's vid-console and the angry face of Morgus appeared on the screen. 'Stotz, why have you disobeyed my orders? I told you to stay in orbit.'

'I'm sorry, sir,' said Stotz wearily. 'The Doctor tricked us. Somehow he got control of the ship, and – '

Morgus cut him short. 'I don't want excuses. I'm on my way to join you. Put out a homing beacon.'

'You're coming here?'

'Yes. My future plans may have to be changed drastically. I am in beta-drive, so expect me shortly.'

'Something wrong?'

The screen went blank. Morgus had broken the connection.

Stotz stared worriedly at the empty screen. He could sense danger.

Chellak and Salateen were leading their advance party towards Sharaz Jek's secret base.

Salateen halted the men at a point where several tunnels met.

Chellak came up beside him. 'Trouble, Major?'

'Not too sure of the route from here, sir. I thought I'd memorised it pretty thoroughly but . . .'

'Take your time.'

'I remember this cave well enough, sir. The vaulted roof, those pillars there. I'd swear we're only a few yards from Sharaz Jek's headquarters now.'

Chellak turned to the men. 'Safety catches off. Stay on the alert.'

'The trouble is, I was coming out of one of those tunnels, and trying to keep an eye on the girl at the same time.'

Chellak produced a chart from his belt-pouch. 'I think we came this way when we first landed. There's a ventilation shaft on the left that runs through to the old refinery. But the rest is unknown territory. We just haven't surveyed this level yet.'

'I'm pretty sure now, sir. It's that opening there,

on the left. I remember dragging the girl over that rock-fall.'

Chellak nodded. 'You'd better go forwards and recce. I'll call Red Force to hold their advance, don't want them leap-frogging us.'

Beckoning to a couple of men to follow him, Salateen moved forwards.

They moved cautiously down the left-hand tunnel. Suddenly an android stepped out in front of them. It surveyed them with the single eye set into the white-domed head.

'Come on, keep moving,' said Salateen quietly. 'It won't fire at the belt-plate.'

They were his last words – the android shot him down.

As Salateen fell dying, his men opened fire. More androids appeared and soon a fierce fire-fight was raging in the narrow tunnels.

Salateen's two men were soon mown down, but by now Chellak's men were moving up the tunnels in force and the androids were blasted in their turn.

Chellak went and knelt beside Salateen's body for a moment. He checked the pulse, but there was no sign of life. Salateen's blue eyes stared sightlessly at the roof of the tunnel.

Gently Chellak closed them. He rose, grim-faced, and led his men forwards.

The burst of energy that had carried the Doctor through his escape from the space-ship was fading now and his weakened body was beginning to tire.

The gun-runners pounded remorselessly after him. They were gaining now, their bullets coming ever closer.

The Doctor found himself running towards an exceptionally steep dune. He began stumbling wearily towards the top, his aching muscles screaming for rest.

He was almost at the top when he stumbled and fell. Rolling over and over he tumbled to the bottom.

For a moment the Doctor lay there in the soft sand, too exhausted even to move. Wearily he struggled to his feet.

A voice said, 'It's all over, Doctor!'

He turned and saw Krelper silhouetted on the top of a nearby dune.

Krelper raised his machine-pistol. It was an easy shot, and the Doctor was too tired to move, let alone run.

Suddenly he heard an ear-splitting crack, a low rumble and a shriek like that of a million whistling tea kettles.

A huge geyser of mud shot up out of the earth, about midway between the Doctor and Krelper.

'Mud burst! Mud burst!' screamed Krelper in panic. 'Let's get back to the ship.'

The gun-runners turned and ran, the Doctor forgotten.

Wearily the Doctor plodded once more to the top of the dune. This time he made it.

On the other side he could see the entrance to the

caves. He stumbled towards them. 'Not enough time,' he muttered. 'Not enough time . . .'

In the caves around Sharaz Jek's HQ a fierce battle was raging between the androids and Chellak's soldiers. The androids were losing, mown down one by one by the swarming soldiers. Now only a few survived.

Chellak was shouting into his transmitter. 'Flag Carrier to Red Force. Do you receive me? Over.'

There was no reply.

Chellak turned to his sergeant. 'Our support group must have hit trouble. Never mind! We'll settle Jek on our own.'

Chellak's troups surged forwards, mowing down the few remaining androids in their path . . .

In his communications room, Sharaz Jek was following the progress of the battle of the charts that filled his screens. The steadily pulsing energy-sources of the androids were in full retreat, forced back by the blurred body-heat traces that represented living troops. One by one the androids' lights were blinking out.

'Chellak has too many soldiers,' muttered Sharaz Jek. 'My androids are being overrun, destroyed.' He flicked a switch. 'Numbers four and nine – fall back to final defence positions.'

Suddenly Chellak heard a low rumbling sound. A panic-stricken soldier ran towards him from the rear. 'There's a mud burst coming, sir!'

Chellak came to a decision. 'No time to go back. We'll have to fight our way forwards. Come on lads, follow me!' The rumbling came closer and the panic-stricken soldiers turned and fled.

Chellak advanced alone.

The Doctor staggered on through the caves, heading for Sharaz Jek's base. As he approached it, he became aware of the steadily increasing sound of gunfire.

He stopped for a moment, leaning against a rock, gasping for breath. 'No time . . . must find Peri.'

The Doctor staggered on.

Dull thumps were shaking the workshop, and Peri lifted her head. 'What's that noise?'

'The start of a mud burst,' whispered Sharaz Jek. 'We shall be safe here.'

Peri said vaguely. 'I thought perhaps the General was bringing up his heavy artillery . . .'

Sharaz Jek paced restlessly to and fro. 'I must go and see if any of my androids can be repaired. We need to hold Chellak back for just a little longer.'

Hurrying into his armoury, Jek snatched a machine-pistol from the wall. 'Just a little longer,' he muttered, 'and the mud burst will sweep them away.' He hurried off, back through the workroom and out through the heavy metal door.

Cautiously he explored the network of caves

around his base. There were signs of battle everywhere around him, and the whole area was littered with bodies, both human and android.

It became clear to Sharaz Jek that the mud burst had erupted just in time to save him. The soldiers had fought their way to the very edge of his secret base. When the mud burst erupted, the survivors must have retreated, leaving dead soldiers and shattered androids behind them.

Sharaz Jek examined one of the less-damaged androids. It was still standing upright, staring ahead, its gun clasped firmly in its hand. But a quick examination proved that the delicate brain-circuitry was damaged beyond repair.

Not that it mattered now. If the soldiers had all pulled back . . .

The ground shook with a nearby eruption, and rocks showered down from the cave roof. Sharaz Jek ducked under an overhanging ledge for protection until the rock-fall was over. He stepped out of cover and saw that not all his attackers had retreated before the mud burst. General Chellak stood facing him, machine-pistol in hand.

'All right, Jek, the war's over. Are you going to surrender?'

'Never!'

Sharaz Jek fired, Chellak ducked, and Sharaz Jek turned and ran.

Chellak hurried after him. He was determined not to lose him now.

* * *

Krelper and Stark were surprised to see a second space-ship, a luxury interplanetary space-yacht, standing beside their battered freighter.

They were even more surprised to find an expensively-dressed, cold-faced stranger, wearing the pigtail of the highest social rank, sitting in Stotz's pilot chair, with Stotz standing deferentially beside him.

Krelper came uncertainly into the control room. 'The mud burst,' he stammered. 'It's started. We'd better get out of here . . .' His voice trailed off as he stared at the man in Stotz's chair. Krelper knew that face. He had seen it on newscasts, amongst the little group of VIPs that always surrounded the President.

'What about the Doctor?' demanded Stotz.

Krelper's eyes were still fixed on the newcomer. 'The Doctor? Oh, we lost him.'

'Lost him?' repeated Morgus coldly. 'Why do you stare at me? Perhaps you think you know me?'

His hand closed round the machine-pistol that lay in his lap.

Hurriedly Krelper shook his head. 'No, sir.'

Stotz grinned. 'Even if he does, Krelper won't say anything.'

'It would be most unwise. Stotz, I want to speak to you alone.'

'Sure,' said Stotz uneasily. 'You two – out!'

'Come on,' muttered Krelper and led his fellow gun-runner away.

When they were gone Morgus said, 'Well, Stotz, no doubt you are wondering why I am here.'

Stotz shrugged. 'You're the boss.'

'Yes. Well, there is a possibility, I wouldn't put it any stronger than that – that my part in all this has been discovered.'

Stotz grinned. 'When you say all this, you mean gun-running, and collecting spectrox and – '

'Exactly,' said Morgus impatiently. 'My conscience is clear. I had to keep the supply of spectrox flowing, and if I hadn't provided Sharaz Jek with arms he would easily have found some other source. But the Praesidium will find my actions treasonable.'

Stotz laughed. 'Yeah ... well, I guess they'd execute all of us – if they could catch us.'

'I have a contingency plan. It is possible that my involvement was suspected only by the President. That is why he sent the Doctor here without telling me. But the President is dead. Now, if he shared his suspicions with anyone else, I shall know within a few hours. In which case, I shall not be able to return to Androzani Major. I have a considerable private fortune invested in other planets in the Sirius system, but when I leave here I want to take with me Jek's private hoard of spectrox. That is the key to unlimited power.'

Stotz laughed harshly. 'Sharaz Jek isn't going to let that go so easily.'

'Perhaps not. But you know where it is, do you not?'

'Well – sort of. It's very close to cave twenty-six on Yellow Level.'

'Before I left Major, Stotz, I was informed that the Army intend to attack Sharaz Jek's headquarters in force tonight. While he is fighting the Army, we could locate the spectrox store. What do you think?'

Stotz considered. 'Maybe. Yellow Level isn't too deep.' He cocked his head at the sound of a distant rumble. 'What about the mud burst?'

'If we go into the caves after the first burst, we should be back here long before the major explosion – as long as we don't have to waste too much time in locating the spectrox store.'

'Yeah, maybe,' said Stotz dubiously. 'But we don't know exactly where in his base Sharaz Jek has stored the stuff.'

'I'm relying on you, Stotz. What about the others?'

'They'll want their cut.'

'If they can carry fifty kilos each,' said Morgus slowly. 'That will mean another hundred to share – between us.'

Stotz glanced towards the door. 'You do mean – between *us*? Just us two?'

'Precisely,' said Morgus.

Stotz smiled, and stroked his machine-pistol.

11

Take-over

As he stumbled on through the caves, the Doctor was vaguely aware that conditions were far from normal. It was hotter for one thing, and every now and again the ground beneath him seemed to shake and tremble.

He was making his way through a long narrow cave littered with standing boulders when he heard a dull roar from somewhere ahead. The sound became louder and louder, as if something huge was moving towards him. A hot wind rushed down the tunnel.

The Doctor spotted a jagged, flat-topped rock close by. He began scaling it with painful effort, flattening himself out as he reached the top.

Suddenly a stream of boiling mud flooded through the caves, pouring over the ground and flying through the air at the same time, forced through the caves under pressure by some vast eruption in the seething planetary core.

The Doctor lay flat, shielding his face, waiting until the mud burst had passed. He scrambled down from his rock and plodded on his way, slipping and stumbling on a rock floor that was now spattered with deposits of steaming mud.

Like some black phantom, Sharaz Jek hurried through the caves, desperate to reach his base before the next mud burst. He reached the corridor outside the workroom at last. Opening the door he went inside. Peri was still laying on her work-bench, wrapped in a blanket.

Tenderly Sharaz Jek lifted her to her feet . . . The door behind him flew open revealing the pursuing Chellak.

Chellak raised his gun to fire. Without letting go of Peri, Sharaz Jek kicked it from his hand.

With a roar of anger Chellak sprang, bearing both Peri and Sharaz Jek to the ground.

The two men grappled fiercely, rolling over and over, while Peri huddled sobbing beneath her blanket.

Fighting with maniacal strength, Sharaz Jek heaved Chellak to his feet, forcing him back towards the open door.

Struggling desperately, Chellak tried to get a grip on Sharaz Jek's throat. His hands slipped upwards, and somehow he tore the mask away from Sharaz Jek's face.

At the sight of the mutilated features Chellak gave a choking scream. His eyes widened in horror and his strength seemed to slip away.

Before he could recover himself, Sharaz Jek

hurled him through the door, closing and locking it behind him.

Chellak picked himself up just in time to hear the rumbling of the mud burst as it surged towards him. He hammered frantically on the door. 'Jek!' he screamed. 'Jek!' But it was too late.

An avalanche of boiling mud poured down the corridor and swept him away.

On the other side of the door, Sharaz Jek staggered over to Peri. She lay crouched on the floor, curled up like a baby, the blanket covering her face.

Tenderly, Sharaz Jek pulled it away. 'Nothing can hurt you now,' he whispered.

Peri opened her eyes – and looked into the unmasked face of Sharaz Jek.

Like Chellak before her, she gave a scream of pure horror. Her reaction struck Sharaz Jek like a blow. Covering his face with his hands he leaped away from her. He scrambled under a workbench and lay there, hunched up and sobbing with misery.

Morgus was about to inform his faithful assistant Krau Timmin, of the change in his plans. Still sitting in Stotz's pilot chair, he punched up the vid-code for his own office.

Krau Timmin appeared on the screen, elegant as ever in her blue business robe, blonde hair immaculately in place.

'Krau Timmin, I would like you to – ' Morgus broke off, staring hard at the screen. 'Krau Timmin, are you sitting at my desk?'

'Yes. This call is on the secret line. I am simply endeavouring to maintain your traditions.'

'Krau Timmin, I don't like your tone – '

Incredibly, she interrupted him. 'I wish that was all I didn't like about you.'

'How dare you speak to me like that? I'll have you punished for this insolence.'

Krau Timmin laughed. 'I don't think so, Morgus. You're finished.'

Morgus glared furiously at the cool figure on the screen. 'What do you mean?'

'Washed up,' explained Krau Timmin kindly. 'Kaput! The Praesidium has issued warrants for your arrest on seventeen counts, ranging from the murder of the President to treason, grand fraud, embezzlement – oh yes, and that little business at Northcawl copper mines. They know about that as well.'

'Falsehoods,' snarled Morgus. 'Fabricated charges, malicious lies. They can't possibly have any proof.'

'It's all fully documented, I'm afraid – and they have an excellent witness.'

'Impossible! Who is this malicious slanderer?'

'Me,' said Krau Timmin coolly.

So comical was the look of astonishment on Morgus's face that Stotz laughed out loud.

'Does that really surprise you, Morgus?' Krau

117

Timmin went on sweetly. 'Do you really think I didn't know what was going on here?'

'You betrayed me?' whispered Morgus. 'After all these years?'

'Think of it this way, Morgus – I deposed you. *I* am now Chairman and Chief Director of the Sirius Conglomerate. Oh, and incidentally, the Government have seized all your private assets, including those secret funds you had salted away on the outer planets. Goodbye, Morgus.'

Abruptly she severed the connection and the screen went blank. For a moment Morgus just sat there stunned.

Then he said fiercely, 'I'm not beaten yet. There is still the spectrox.' He looked round the control room. 'There are four of us here, more than enough to handle Jek.' He stood up. 'Now, pick up your guns and let's go.'

Nobody moved.

'Did you hear what I said? Let's move!'

'We ain't going anywhere,' said Krelper. 'Except maybe back to Major.'

'I've paid you well for these trips. Now, do as I say.'

Krelper shook his head. 'The way we see it, we already got two kilos of spectrox. That's enough for us.'

'Two kilos!' sneered Morgus. 'I tell you, Jek's got tons of it stored away.'

'Yeah? Well, we ain't getting our heads blown off by Jek's dummies, or boiled alive in that mud. Not for twenty tons we·ain't.'

Morgus glared furiously at them. 'You cowardly miserable curs!' He swung round. 'What about you, Stotz? Are you staying here with this gutter trash?'

Stotz hesitated for a moment. Then he rose, picking up his gun. 'I'll go with you, Morgus. I've got a few old scores to settle with Sharaz Jek.'

Morgus strode out of the control room, and Stotz followed him. He stopped in the doorway, smiling, raising a hand in salute. 'Bye, Krelper.' Krelper nodded, and Stotz went out of the control room.

The two gun-runners heard the outer door open and close.

Krelper hurried towards the pilot chair but before he reached it he heard a gasp from Stark. Swinging round, he saw Stotz in the control room doorway, machine-pistol raised.

Before Krelper could move or speak, Stotz fired a staccato burst, mowing him down. A second burst disposed of Stark.

Stotz turned and left the ship.

The Doctor staggered on through the caves, stumbling and sliding on the mud-smeared rocky floor.

He slipped, going down an incline, picked himself up and found himself looking at the legs of an android. The Doctor looked up, expecting the muzzle of the machine-pistol to swing round towards him. But the android ignored him, staring over his head.

It was standing on a ledge, a little higher than the Doctor, and as he watched, it toppled slowly forwards. The Doctor jumped aside as the android crashed to the ground.

He examined it briefly: there was a line of bullet holes across its chest. Clearly there had been some kind of battle . . .

The Doctor moved on.

Not far away, two oddly-assorted colleagues were picking their way through the mud. Stotz and Morgus were crossing a great cave filled with standing boulders.

Stotz came to a sudden halt. Morgus looked at him impatiently. 'Stotz, you must lead. You know the way.'

Calmly, Stotz sat down on a convenient rock. 'Sure! But before we go any further, Morgus, let's get a couple of things straight.'

'What kind of things?'

Stotz grinned insolently at him. 'An hour ago you were the boss. Now that's all changed. You're the same as me now.' Stotz slapped his machine-pistol. 'A man with a gun.'

Morgus stared at him in genuine astonishment. 'I, the same as you? I am Morgus! I am descended from the first colonists.'

'You're wanted for murder and treason. You're on the run, Morgus!'

'And you are wasting time, Stotz.'

Stotz was enjoying his new-found equality. 'You want me to help you, right? Well, if we do happen to come out of this with any spectrox, there's going to be none of that four parts for you and one for me stuff. We split right down the middle, all right?'

'Of course. Now lead the way.'

Satisfied that he had the upper hand, Stotz moved on.

Morgus shot a glance of burning hatred at his retreating back. It was intolerable to be obliged to negotiate with such scum. But of course, it was only temporary. Once the spectrox was safely in Morgus's hands, he would have no further need for Stotz . . .

The Doctor hammered desperately on the door to the workroom. 'Sharaz Jek! Let me in!'

Somewhat to his surprise the door swung open, revealing the masked figure of Sharaz Jek, cradling Peri in his arms. The Doctor went inside.

Sharaz Jek began walking up and down, cradling the unconscious Peri like a child. 'She is so beautiful,' he crooned. 'So beautiful . . . so beautiful!'

It was immediately clear to the Doctor that Sharaz Jek's grip on sanity, never very secure, was slipping rapidly.

'How is she, Jek?'

'She is dying, Doctor. She has spectrox toxaemia.'

'I know,' said the Doctor briefly. Taking Peri from Jek's arms, he laid her gently on a work-bench, and examined her. Her face was flushed and her temperature incredibly high.

The Doctor plucked the stick of celery from his lapel and squeezed it under Peri's nose.

Peri opened her eyes. 'Celery soup . . .'

121

'Come on, Peri,' said the Doctor urgently.

She smiled. 'Hello, Doctor.'

'That's more like it.'

'Goodbye, Doctor,' said Peri faintly and closed her eyes.

'No, no, Peri, don't give up. You mustn't give up.'

Frantically the Doctor waved the crushed celery under her nose.

'What is that?' asked Jek curiously.

'Celery. It's a powerful restorative where I come from. Unfortunately the human olfactory system is comparatively feeble.' The Doctor tossed the celery aside. 'You know of the cure that Professor Jackij discovered?'

'The milk of the queen bat? Of course! But the dormant queens cannot be reached, Doctor. There's little air in those levels.'

'It's her only chance. Do you know where the queens can be found?'

Jek strode to a console and punched up a computer map on a read-out screen. 'Of course. When I first came here my androids surveyed and mapped the whole system. If only my Salateen android were here, I could send him down, possibly save her life.'

The Doctor was studying the map. 'I'm going down there. Now, show me the best route.'

Jek's finger-hand moved across the screen. 'The place you want is here, the great ravine. It's two hundred metres down, but you'll collapse before you get there.'

'I can store oxygen for several minutes, far longer than any human.' The Doctor went back to Peri. 'Meanwhile you must do everything you can to keep her temperature down until I get back.'

'Of course.'

The Doctor nodded and headed for the door.

'Wait, Doctor,' called Sharaz Jek. 'I have just one oxygen cylinder left. I used it when I went into the baking chambers of the refinery. It will run out in minutes, but it may help.'

He took a little hand cylinder from a high shelf and held it out. 'You will need some kind of container . . .' He searched another shelf and found a small glass phial.

As he took the cylinder and the phial from Sharaz Jek's hand it occurred to the Doctor that it was strange how quickly their mutual concern for Peri's life had made them allies. It also occurred to him that if by some miracle he did save Peri's life, not to mention his own, he would have to kill Sharaz Jek in order to take Peri away from him.

Still, that was for the future — if they had one.

With a last look at Peri, the Doctor hurried from the workshop.

Scarcely aware that he had gone, Sharaz Jek hovered in anguish over the unconscious girl.

What was it the Doctor had said? Keep her cool, keep her temperature down . . .

He had switched off the extractor fans before the attack to help safeguard the precise location of his HQ. There was no need for such caution now . . .

123

Hurrying to an instrument panel, Jek pulled a lever. The motors hummed into life.

Jek hurried back to Peri. He crouched beside her, stroking her burning forehead with his scarred hand . . .

12

Change

Morgus and Stotz groped their way through the steam-fog that hung in the air of the caves after the mud burst. Everything looked different, and it was hard for Stotz to get his bearings. He pointed to a ladder half-buried in mud. 'I think this is cave twenty-six Yellow Level, where we met Jek.'

Suddenly he caught the glint of a silver uniform ahead. 'Duck!'

They crouched down behind an angle of rock.

Stotz peered out. There were uniforms right enough, but the soldiers who wore them were dead, their bodies mingled with those of the shattered androids. He straightened up. 'Looks like the Army got here first.'

Morgus looked at the body-strewn cave without emotion. 'I didn't hear any firing.'

'I reckon the firing's over.'

'Where to now?' asked Morgus.

'Down to Blue Level. From there – well, in these

conditions, it's anybody's guess. But that's where Jek came from, so let's go.'

The Doctor had come across a body too, but it wasn't human, or even android.

He found what looked like an immense mud-covered boulder, half-blocking a narrow tunnel. Working his way around it, he suddenly realised that it wasn't a boulder at all, but the dead body of the magma creature. It must have been caught in the path of the mud burst and either choked or boiled to death. The monster's eyes were glazed and the mouth gaped open, showing rows of enormous, savage fangs.

A little hysterically, the Doctor patted the great horned head. 'It's not your lucky day either, is it?'

He hurried on his way.

Down on Blue Level, Stotz and Morgus were lost. The fog and the darkness and the mud seemed to have transformed everything, and Stotz found that his memory of his one brief visit to Sharaz Jek's workroom was of little use to him.

'Which way?' demanded Morgus impatiently.

'I'm not sure . . .' There was a distant rumbling and Stotz cocked his head uneasily. 'Come on, Morgus, we've got to get out of here. That main mud burst can't be far away.'

Morgus held up his hand. 'Listen, what is that?'

Stotz listened. This time he heard not the rumble of the mud burst but a deep powerful hum.

He grinned savagely. 'Sounds like a motor – we must be close! Come on, Morgus. This way!'

The Doctor had reached the edge of the great ravine. Here at the lowest level of the caves was a deep underground chasm, its bubbling seething depths filled with the scalding magma.

There were ledges on the side of the ravine, and here in crannies and alcoves the great queen bats hung in their long hibernation.

It was very hot and the air was thin, almost too thin to breathe. The Doctor knew he had little time. Refreshing himself with a quick breath of oxygen, he climbed over the edge of the ravine and began working his way downwards.

The surface was irregular and treacherous. There were hand-holds that crumbled, paths and ledges that disappeared . . .

It was a kind of vertical maze . . .

Slowly, inch by inch, the Doctor worked his way downwards, aware that at any moment one slip would plunge him to his death in the scalding magma below.

At last he found what he was looking for. In a deep crevice in the rock face an immense black shape hung upside down, leather wings wrapped about it like a great cape.

The Doctor studied the creature in astonishment. It was immense, over five feet long, and broad in proportion. The Doctor hoped it was thoroughly dormant. He felt too weak to wrestle with a normal bat, let alone one this size.

Edging his way into the cleft, he worked his way round to the front of the creature's body, feeling for the milk-glands on the thorax.

When he had located them, he took the glass phial from his pocket, removed the stopper and began squeezing the precious milky liquid into the container.

To his relief, the queen bat suffered his attentions, more or less unperturbed. A huge, glowing green eye opened for a moment and surveyed him unblinkingly.

The eye closed, and the queen bat slept on.

Gently the Doctor continued with his task.

There was just enough of the precious fluid to fill the little flask. Squeezing out the last few drops, the Doctor stoppered the phial and put it carefully in his pocket.

He took out Sharaz Jek's cylinder and refreshed himself with another quick burst of oxygen. This time the cylinder hissed for a few seconds and then expired.

Tossing it into the seething mud below, the Doctor gathered his energies for the long and dangerous climb to the top of the ravine . . .

Sharaz Jek hovered at Peri's side in a frenzy, wringing out fresh cloths to bathe her forehead, stroking her hair, holding her apparently lifeless hands.

'Peri,' he whispered. 'Peri, can you hear me?'

Her eyelids fluttered and she moaned faintly.

It was clear to Sharaz Jek that for all his efforts she was sinking ever deeper into a coma that could only end in her death . . .

Absorbed in his task, Sharaz Jek did not hear the door opening behind him.

Stotz and Morgus came into the room, machine-pistols in their hands. At the sight of Sharaz Jek, Stotz raised his weapon to fire, but Morgus knocked it aside.

Sensing movement behind him, Sharaz Jek whirled round, to find himself covered by Morgus's machine-pistol.

'Jek! Where is the spectrox?'

Only one person in the universe was more important to Sharaz Jek at that moment than Peri – and that was his old enemy.

Sharaz Jek's eyes widened. 'Morgus!'

He took a pace towards him.

Morgus stepped back. 'Take one more step and we shoot.'

As far as Sharaz Jek was concerned, the machine-pistol in Morgus's hand could have been a flower or a fan.

'Do you think bullets could stop me?' he said softly. Suddenly his voice rose to an impassioned shout. 'You stinking offal, Morgus – *look at me!*'

He reached up and pulled off his face-mask.

For a moment both Stotz and Morgus stared in horror at the two mad eyes blazing from a face that was no more than a formless blob, a lump of peeling corrugated skin, devoid of all features.

Then Sharaz Jek sprang, knocking Stotz to the ground. He took hold of Morgus, seizing him by the throat. The gun fell from Morgus's hands as Sharaz Jek began throttling the life out of him.

Picking himself up, Stotz hovered around the edge of the struggle, looking for a clear shot at Jek.

Sharaz Jek bent Morgus backwards over a work-bench, growling like a beast as his hands tightened on Morgus's throat. Setting his pistol to single-fire, Stotz took careful aim and pumped bullet after bullet into Sharaz Jek's back.

Suddenly there were more shots. Stotz staggered under some tremendous blow.

He turned and saw the Salateen android in the doorway. Stotz stared wide-eyed as the android fired, again and again. Still not quite realising what was happening to him, Stotz crashed to the floor.

None of this distracted Sharaz Jek from his one overriding concern – the strangling of Morgus. Ignoring his own terrible wounds, he squeezed the throat of his enemy until the body went limp in his hands.

Lifting the body high, Sharaz Jek hurled it into a bench packed with complex electronic equipment. The equipment exploded in flames and Morgus lay dead amidst the blaze.

Sharaz Jek staggered and turned.

A voice said, 'Master.' It was the Salateen android, his greatest creation.

Jek staggered towards it. 'Hold me,' he ordered hoarsely, and fell into the android's arms, slipping to his knees.

Leaning forward, the android held the dying body.

The door opened and the Doctor staggered into the room. As single-minded in his way as Sharaz Jek, the Doctor lifted the unconscious Peri in his arms, and carried her from the blazing workshop.

Calm amidst the chaos of smoke and flame and exploding equipment, the Salateen-android stood motionless, holding the body of its master.

The journey through the caves was an unending nightmare. As he staggered onwards the Doctor was vaguely aware that once again the whole cave system was shaking and trembling. Another mud burst was on the way – the big one.

Somehow he reached the surface at last.

All at once he was staggering across the shallow desert basin, the TARDIS shimmering like a mirage on the other side.

The ground was shaking. Every now and again great mud fountains jetted like liquid volcanoes out of the ground. The Doctor ignored them. His task was almost over now.

When he reached the door of the TARDIS, the Doctor put Peri down, very carefully, and fumbled in his pocket for the key.

His fingers were shaking and somehow the little phial of bat-milk came out of his pocket at the same time. It fell to the ground, the stopper jarred loose, and the milky liquid began running away in the sand.

The Doctor's hand whipped out and snatched up the phial. It was more than half-empty. Picking up the stopper, the Doctor closed the phial and put it very carefully back in his pocket.

Somehow he got the TARDIS door open and dragged Peri inside. Leaving her huddled on the control room floor, he staggered up to the console and set the controls for take-off.

Outside, the desert ground was trembling now, and the huge mud geysers were everywhere.

As the TARDIS faded away, a huge volcano of mud erupted on the spot where it had stood just seconds before.

The Doctor watched the steady rise and fall of the time rotor, then slid gently to the ground.

For a moment he lay still. Then, realising that his task was still not completed, he began crawling determinedly towards Peri.

When he reached her he took out the little phial, unstoppered it with shaking fingers, and held it to her lips.

'Peri,' he whispered. 'Peri, can you hear me? Open your mouth. You must drink this . . .'

Peri's mouth opened, just a little.

The Doctor tilted her head back and poured the entire contents of the phial between her lips. Then he sank back, exhausted.

He lay there for a moment, quite contented, staring at the TARDIS ceiling.

Everything seemed strange, unreal. He could feel the TARDIS control room slipping away from him.

'Is this death?' said the Doctor wonderingly.

'Doctor? What's happening?' called a familiar voice.

Suddenly the Doctor became aware that someone was shaking him. He opened his eyes and saw Peri. She looked, under the circumstances, quite remarkably well.

The Doctor smiled. 'Ah, Peri, you're better . . . I see Professor Jackij knew his stuff.'

Peri stared at him, still a little dazed.

After a nightmare of shouts, and shots and flames, she had woken to find herself back in the TARDIS, a little weak but apparently quite cured.

Suddenly the memories came flooding back. 'Jackij! You got the bat's milk?'

The Doctor nodded. 'Contains an anti-vesicant, I imagine,' he said brightly. 'Interesting!'

'Where is it?' demanded Peri.

'What?'

'The bat's milk!'

'Finished,' said the Doctor simply. 'Only enough for you.'

Peri stared at him in horror. 'No, Doctor. No! There must be something I can do. Tell me.'

'Too late, Peri,' said the Doctor calmly. 'Time to say goodbye.'

'Don't give up,' begged Peri. 'You can't leave me now.'

'I might regenerate,' said the Doctor thoughtfully. 'I don't know. Feels – different, this time . . .'

Suddenly the Doctor was nowhere, no-time, suspended in a kind of limbo.

Familiar faces appeared, floated towards him. They spoke.

'What was it you always told me, Doctor?' said Tegan. 'Brave heart! You'll survive.'

Turlough was there. 'You must survive. Too many of your enemies would rejoice in your death.'

Kamelion appeared. 'Turlough speaks the truth, Doctor.'

'You're needed, you mustn't die,' said Nyssa.

'You know that, Doctor,' said Adric reprovingly.

'Adric!' The Doctor frowned. It was nice of all his old friends to come and see him, but surely Adric shouldn't be there.

Adric was dead.

But then, perhaps he was dead himself, thought the Doctor. That would account for it.

Another face appeared, driving away all the others. An evil satanic face with slanting eyebrows and a pointed beard.

The Master.

'No, my dear Doctor, you must die! Die, Doctor! Die, Doctor. Die!'

The Master's face grew to enormous size. He threw back his head and laughed and laughed . . .

Perhaps the Master's taunts affected the Doctor even more than the appeals of his old companions. The one thing the Doctor had never done in all his lives was to let the Master have the last laugh.

Reality split, fragmented, shattered into a thousand pieces, a million choices.

Somehow amongst them all the Doctor chose survival.

Peri blinked – and in that blinking of an eye there was a different Doctor in the TARDIS.

He wore the previous Doctor's clothes, but not his face.

Peri peered cautiously at the newcomer. He had a broad, high forehead and a mop of curly light-brown hair. There was something cat-like about the eyes, a touch of arrogance in the mouth.

'Doctor?' said Peri in astonishment.

'You were expecting someone else?' The voice was clipped, precise, with a definite edge to it.

Peri stammered, 'I . . . I . . . I . . .'

'Three I's in one breath? Makes you sound a rather egotistical young lady!'

Peri stared at him. 'What's happened?'

'Change,' said the Doctor – the new Doctor. 'Change, my dear. And, it seems, not a moment too soon!'

DOCTOR WHO

0426114558	TERRANCE DICKS **Doctor Who and The** **Abominable Snowmen**	**£1.35**
0426200373	**Doctor Who and The** **Android Invasion**	**£1.25**
0426201086	**Doctor Who and The** **Androids of Tara**	**£1.35**
0426116313	IAN MARTER **Doctor Who and The** **Ark in Space**	**£1.35**
0426201043	TERRANCE DICKS **Doctor Who and The** **Armageddon Factor**	**£1.35**
0426112954	**Doctor Who and The** **Auton Invasion**	**£1.50**
0426116747	**Doctor Who and The** **Brain of Morbius**	**£1.35**
0426110250	**Doctor Who and The** **Carnival of Monsters**	**£1.35**
042611471X	MALCOLM HULKE **Doctor Who and** **The Cave Monsters**	**£1.50**
0426117034	TERRANCE DICKS **Doctor Who and The** **Claws of Axos**	**£1.35**
042620123X	DAVID FISHER **Doctor Who and The** **Creature from the Pit**	**£1.35**
0426113160	DAVID WHITAKER **Doctor Who and The Crusaders**	**£1.50**
0426200616	BRIAN HAYLES **Doctor Who and The Curse** **of Peladon**	**£1.50**
0426114639	GERRY DAVIS **Doctor Who and The Cybermen**	**£1.50**
0426113322	BARRY LETTS **Doctor Who and The Daemons**	**£1.50**

Prices are subject to alteration

DOCTOR WHO

	DAVID WHITAKER **Doctor Who and The** **Daleks**	
0426101103		£1.50
	TERRANCE DICKS **Doctor Who and The Dalek** **Invasion of Earth**	
042611244X		£1.35
	Doctor Who and The Day **of the Daleks**	
0426103807		£1.35
	Doctor Who – Death to **the Daleks**	
042620042X		£1.35
	Doctor Who and The **Deadly Assassin**	
0426119657		£1.35
	Doctor Who and The **Destiny of the Daleks**	
0426200969		£1.35
	MALCOLM HULKE **Doctor Who and The** **Dinosaur Invasion**	
0426108744		£1.35
	Doctor Who and **The Doomsday Weapon**	
0426103726		£1.35
	IAN MARTER **Doctor Who and The** **Enemy of the World**	
0426201464		£1.35
	TERRANCE DICKS **Doctor Who and The** **Face of Evil**	
0426200063		£1.35
	ANDREW SMITH **Doctor Who – Full Circle**	
0426201507		£1.35
	TERRANCE DICKS **Doctor Who and The** **Genesis of the Daleks**	
0426112601		£1.35
0426112792	**Doctor Who and The Giant Robot**	£1.35
	MALCOLM HULKE **Doctor Who and The** **Green Death**	
0426115430		£1.35

Prices are subject to alteration

STAR Books are obtainable from many booksellers and newsagents. If you have any difficulty please send purchase price plus postage on the scale below to:

> **Star Cash Sales**
> **P.O. Box 11**
> **Falmouth**
> **Cornwall**
> OR
> **Star Book Service,**
> **G.P.O. Box 29,**
> **Douglas,**
> **Isle of Man,**
> **British Isles.**

While every effort is made to keep prices low, it is sometimes necessary to increase prices at short notice. Star Books reserve the right to show new retail prices on covers which may differ from those advertised in the text or elsewhere.

Postage and Packing Rate
UK: 55p for the first book, 22p for the second book and 14p for each additional book ordered to a maximum charge of £1.75p. BFPO and EIRE: 55p for the first book, 22p for the second book, 14p per copy for the next 7 books, thereafter 8p per book. Overseas: £1.00p for the first book and 25p per copy for each additional book.